Lady Lucy's Ghost Quest

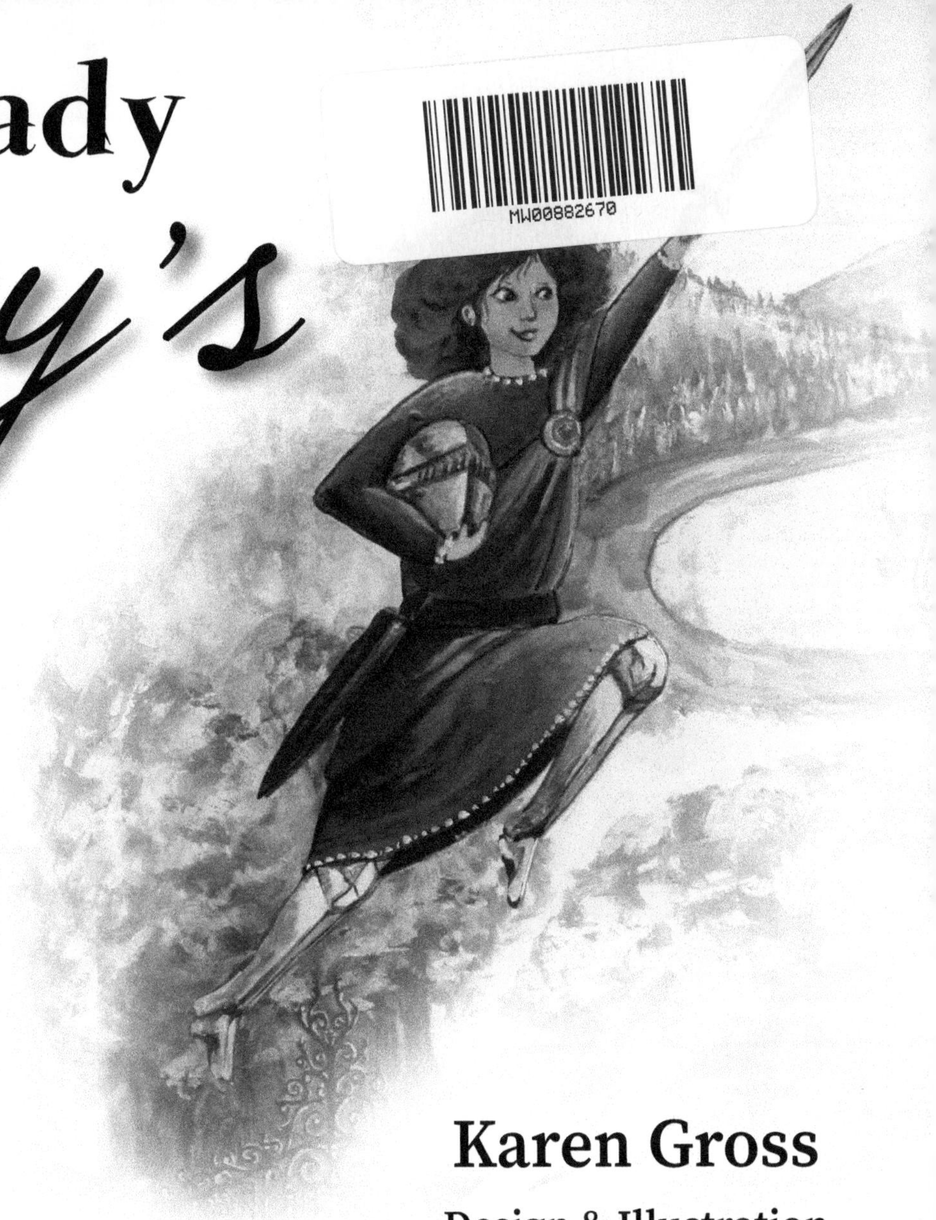

Karen Gross

Design & Illustration
by Dianne Sunda
& Georgia Hamp

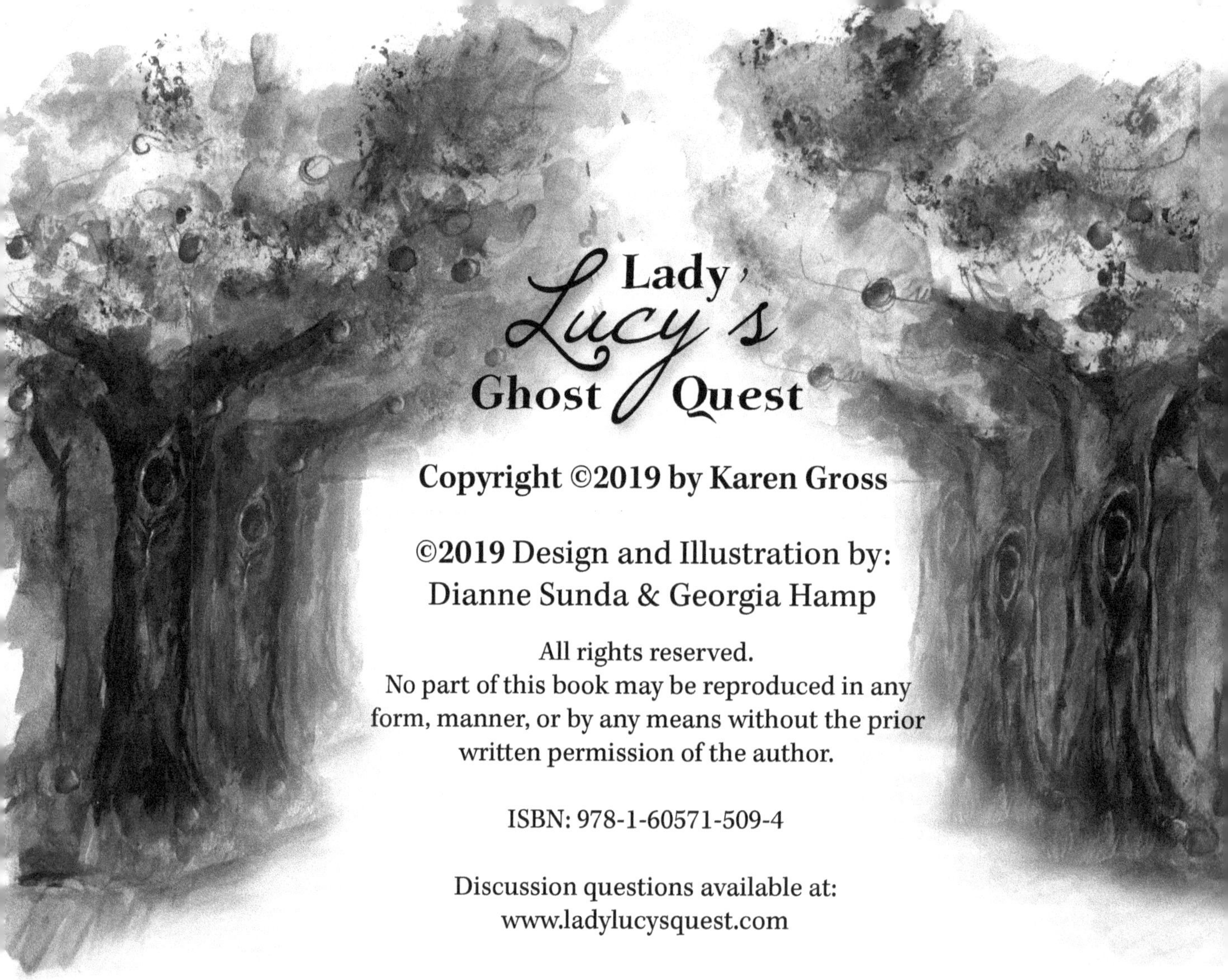

Lady Lucy's Ghost Quest

©2019 Design and Illustration by:
Dianne Sunda & Georgia Hamp

ISBN: 978-1-60571-509-4

Discussion questions available at:
www.ladylucysquest.com

SHIRES PRESS
Manchester Center,
VT 05255
www.northshire.com

Printed in the United States of America

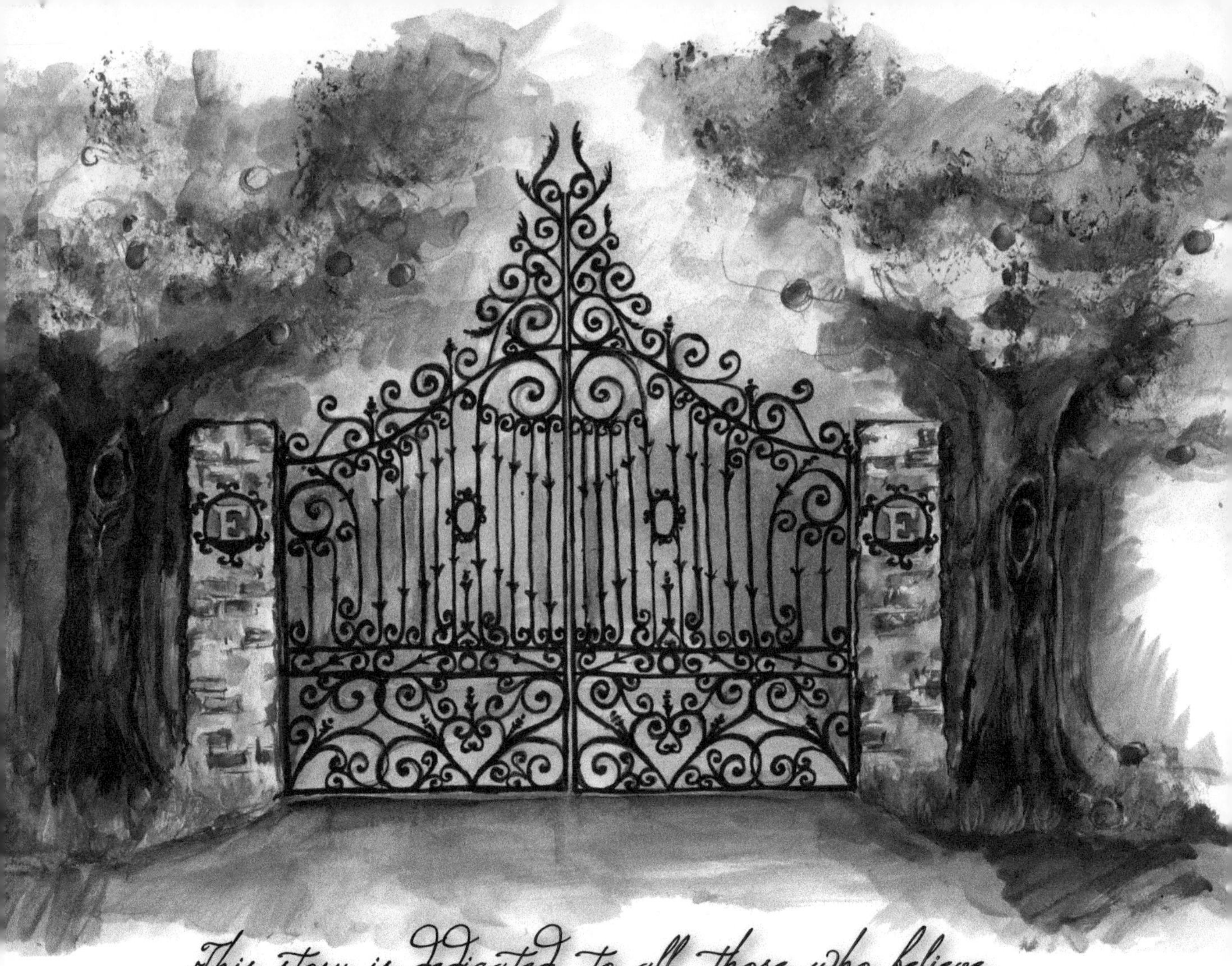

This story is dedicated to all those who believe in the power of the possible, including the power of a phoenix to rise from the ashes or a ghost to guide the way forward.

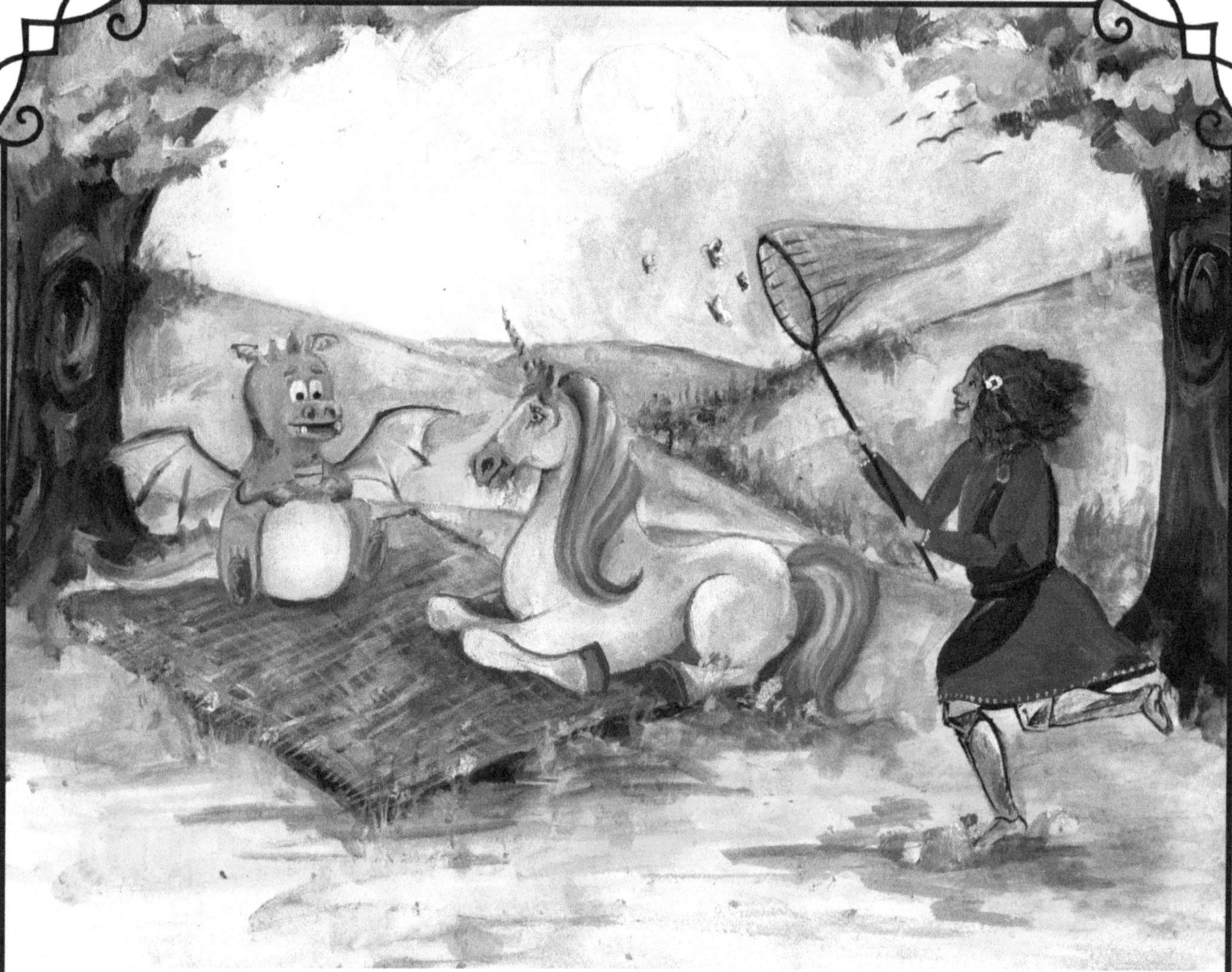

Lady *Lucy*, Dillon (the Dragon) and Tapestry (the Unicorn) were enjoying the summer sun in the County of Heraldshire.

There had been peace in the Kingdom for several seasons and Lady *Lucy* was pleased to be able to spend time with her animal friends; together they maintained the beauty of the Dangerous Dark Forest.

She also spent time helping the young children in the Kingdom experience the joys of the outdoors and she always made sure the children had time to play with Dillon and Tapestry, something that made children, townspeople and other Knights across the Kingdom smile.

Lady *Lucy's* summer calm was interrupted when Squire Saunders arrived at her home with a message from Sir Winston, the oldest and wisest knight in the Kingdom. After a trumpet salutation, the squire read Sir Winston's decree aloud to Lady *Lucy*, Dillon and Tapestry:

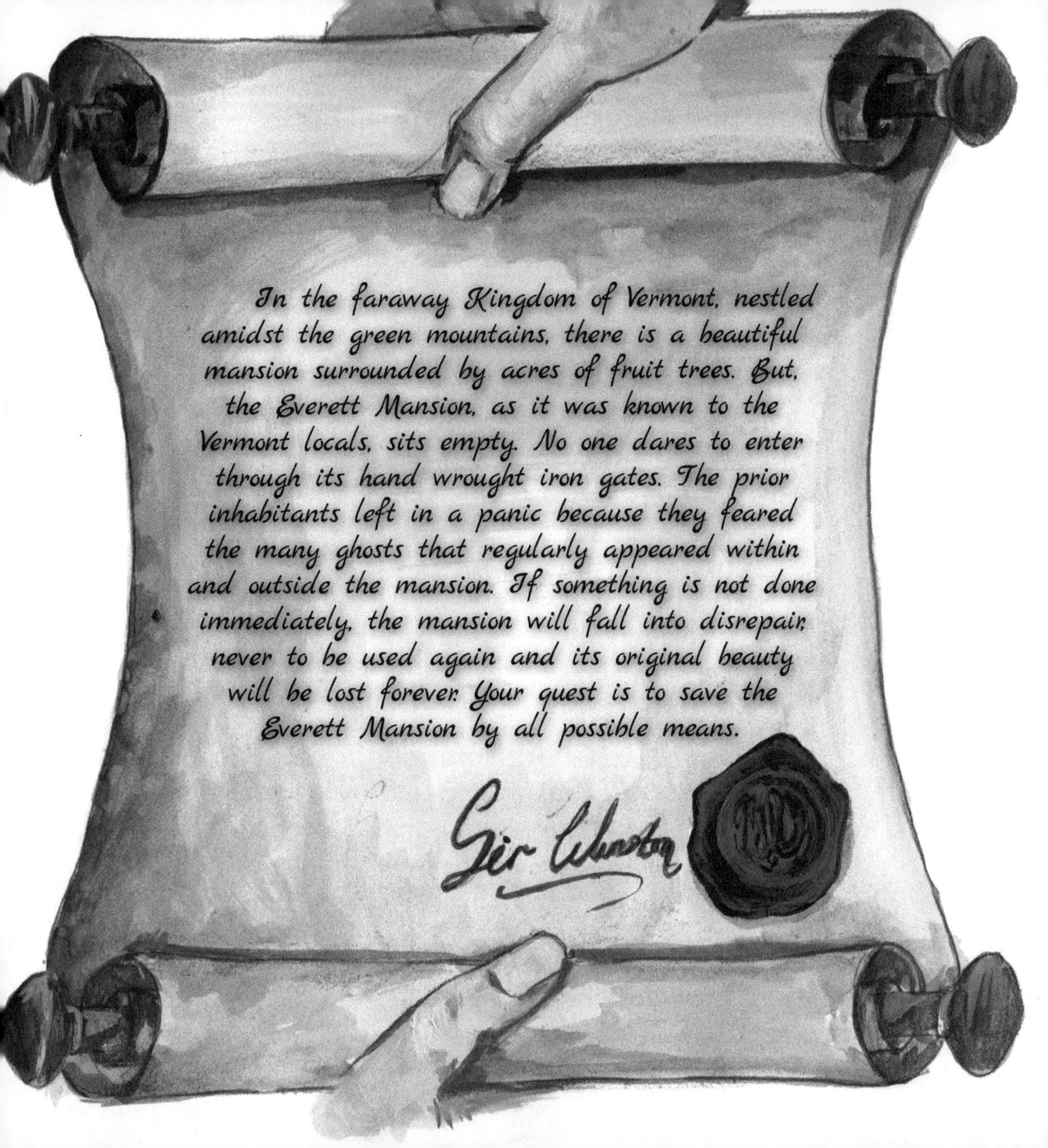
In the faraway Kingdom of Vermont, nestled amidst the green mountains, there is a beautiful mansion surrounded by acres of fruit trees. But, the Everett Mansion, as it was known to the Vermont locals, sits empty. No one dares to enter through its hand wrought iron gates. The prior inhabitants left in a panic because they feared the many ghosts that regularly appeared within and outside the mansion. If something is not done immediately, the mansion will fall into disrepair, never to be used again and its original beauty will be lost forever. Your quest is to save the Everett Mansion by all possible means.

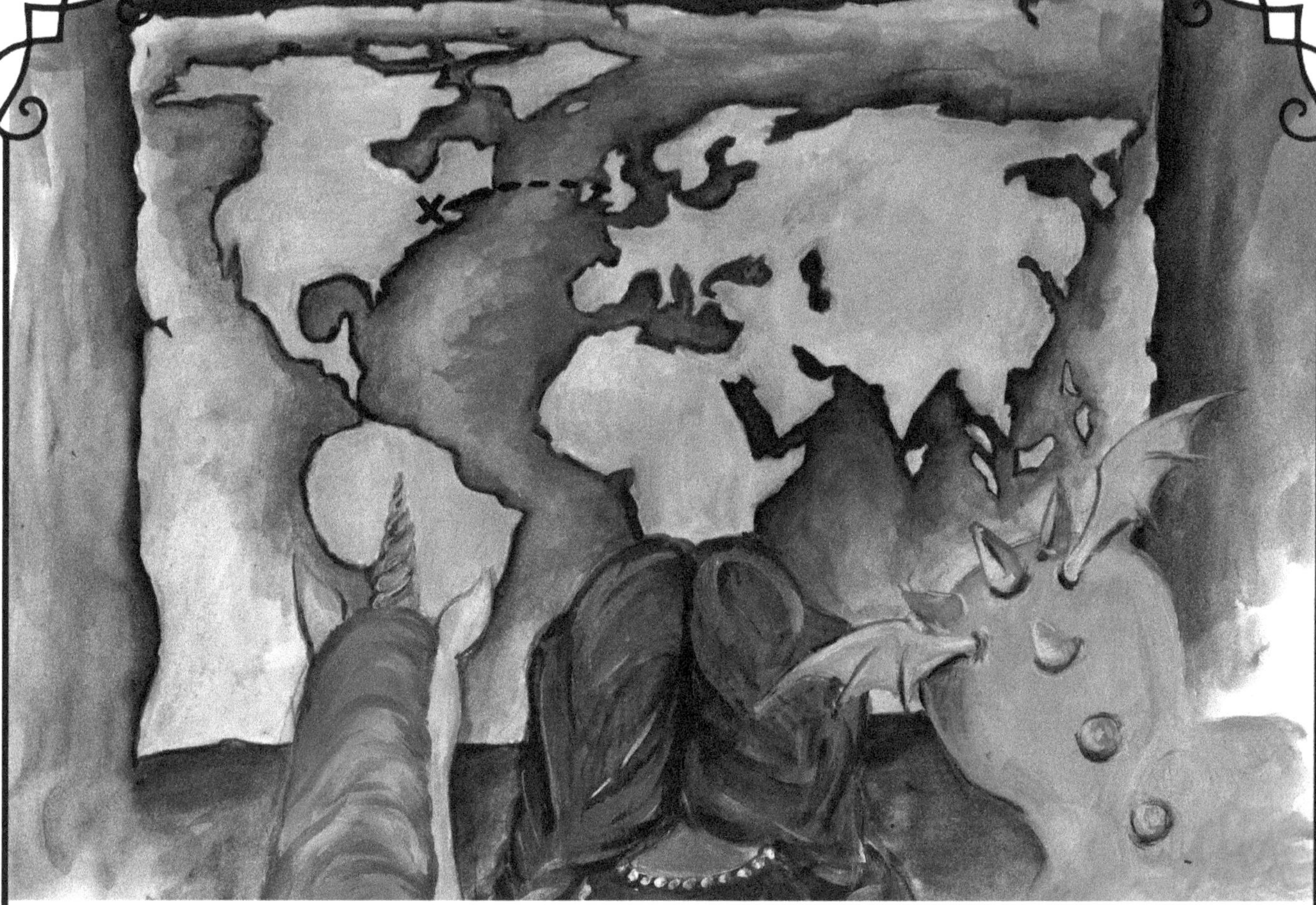

Lady *Lucy*, Dillon and Tapestry immediately went to the castle library to find a map of this faraway place called Vermont. Upon seeing its location, they realized that would take them many days and nights, including over big bodies of water, to get there. If they wanted to save the mansion, they had to depart immediately; there was not a minute to waste.

As they started to pack for the travel ahead, Tapestry scuffed her hoof into the ground, which was always a sign of her being distressed or worried. Lady *Lucy* and Dillon asked, "Tapestry, what's bothering you about this amazing journey to save the mansion? Are you scared of the long travel? Are you scared of going in a boat over the water? Are you scared of getting lost?"

Tapestry shook her multicolored main and tail: "No, none of that bothers me. I'm bothered by one thing – ghosts." Just saying that, her body shook and her ears quivered and her eyes flickered.

Lady *Lucy* and Dillon decided to talk to Sir Winston to find out more about the ghosts at the mansion. Were they all scary? Was there such a thing as a friendly ghost? Were ghosts even real or just the sign of an active imagination?

Sir Winston pulled out a big book sitting on his desk titled *The History of Ghosts* and read this description of ghosts to Lady *Lucy* and Dillon. Tapestry was there too but she was covering her ears.

Ghosts come in all shapes and sizes and they have existed for centuries. Ghosts can move through solid objects; they can slam and open doors; they can turn on lights and blow out candles; they can throw objects across the room. They can scream and whistle. Some say ghosts are the spirit of those who have died who come back to scare or punish living creatures.

"Yipes," said Lady *Lucy*. "Yeek," said Dillon. Tapestry was stunned into silence. Sir Winston then turned to them and said, "Wait. There is more to read on the next page of this big book."

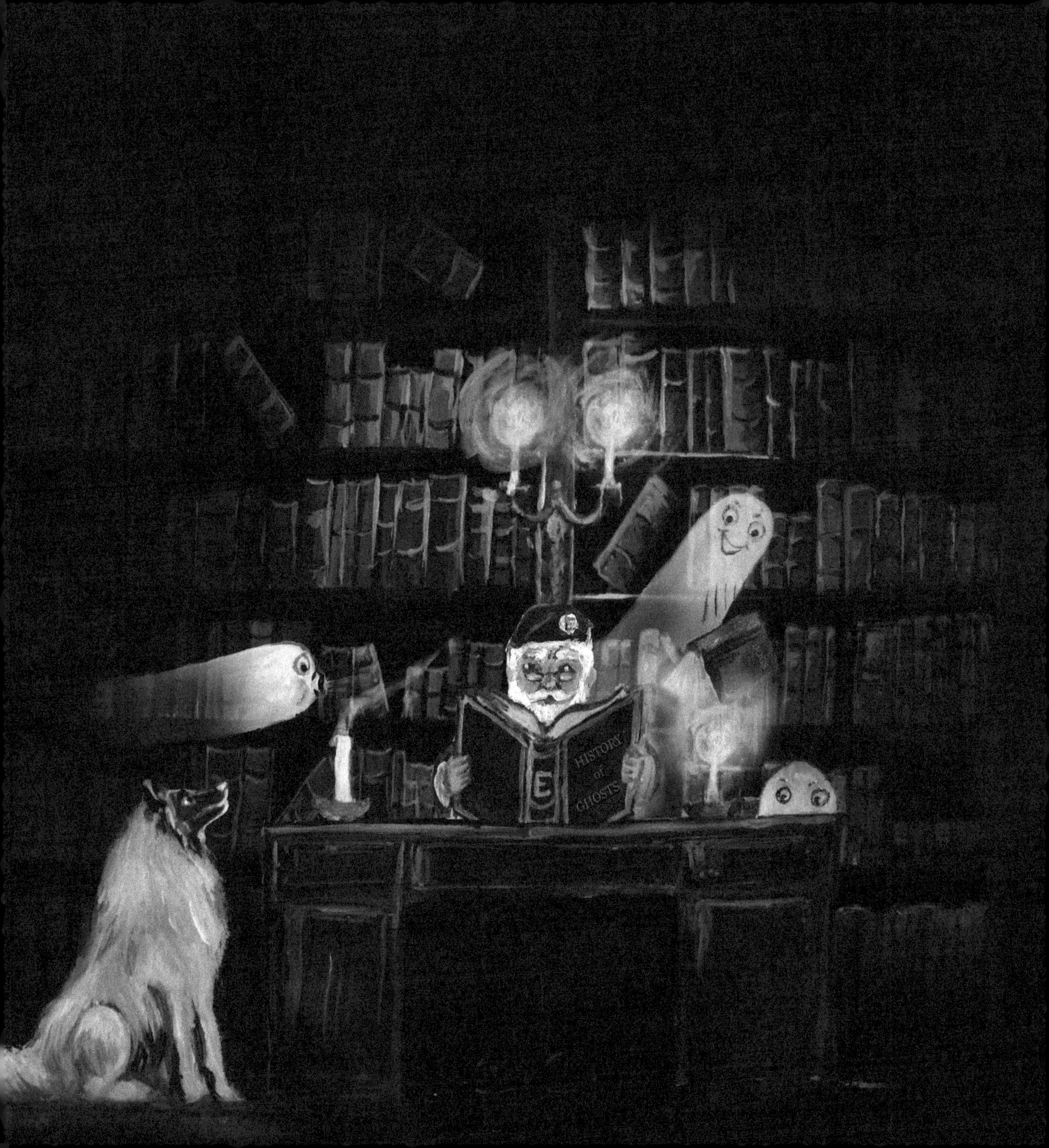
HISTORY of GHOSTS

Sir Winston moved closer to the big book and pulled his glasses down over his nose so he could read more clearly. Loudly and clearly and with expression, Sir Winston read:

Not all ghosts are out for revenge; some ghosts are friendly, and they can even be helpful. They can clean up dirty rooms; they can lead you to hidden treasure; they prevent objects from falling on your head; they guide you in the dark; they even join you for festive events, dancing and playing piano and singing for all to hear. They can guide you to wise decisions.

"Phew," said Lady *Lucy*. "Yippee," said Dillon. Tapestry remained silent, wondering to herself if the book was being truthful. Noting the concern, Sir Winston said, "We would not be sending you to Everett Mansion if we thought you would be hurt and endangered. Instead, we think that, working together, you can restore the mansion to its original glory. Use your imaginations; use your creativity; use your courage."

Emboldened by Sir Winston's words of confidence, Lady *Lucy*, Dillon and Tapestry set out for Vermont and the Everett Mansion. Their journey was remarkable and without incident, and they enjoyed the scenery and each other's company. They were not the only travelers across the big ocean; there were many glorious ships sailing over the water, some catching enormous fish as they went and others using brightly colored sails to speed their travel. The sunsets and sunrises were dramatic in their colors and signaled the passage of time.

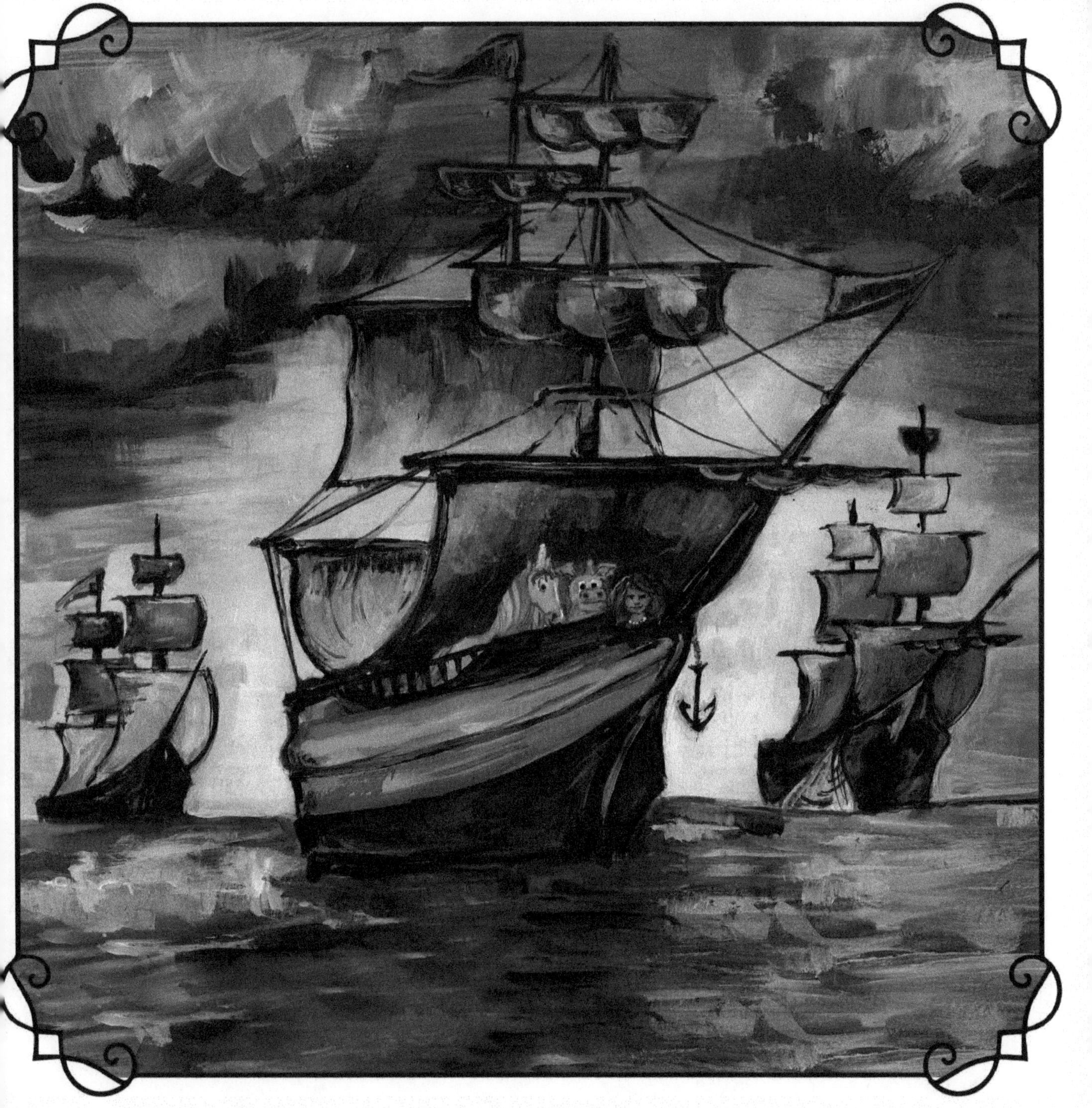

A horse and buggy were at the dock awaiting their arrival. The only problem was that Dillon did not fit in the buggy and Tapestry wanted to be up with the horse, whom she perceived as a new friend, leading the way to Vermont. So, with some rearranging and reorganizing, the threesome from the County of Heraldshire set off to Vermont and the Everett Mansion, unsure of what awaited them but sure in their capacity to do good.

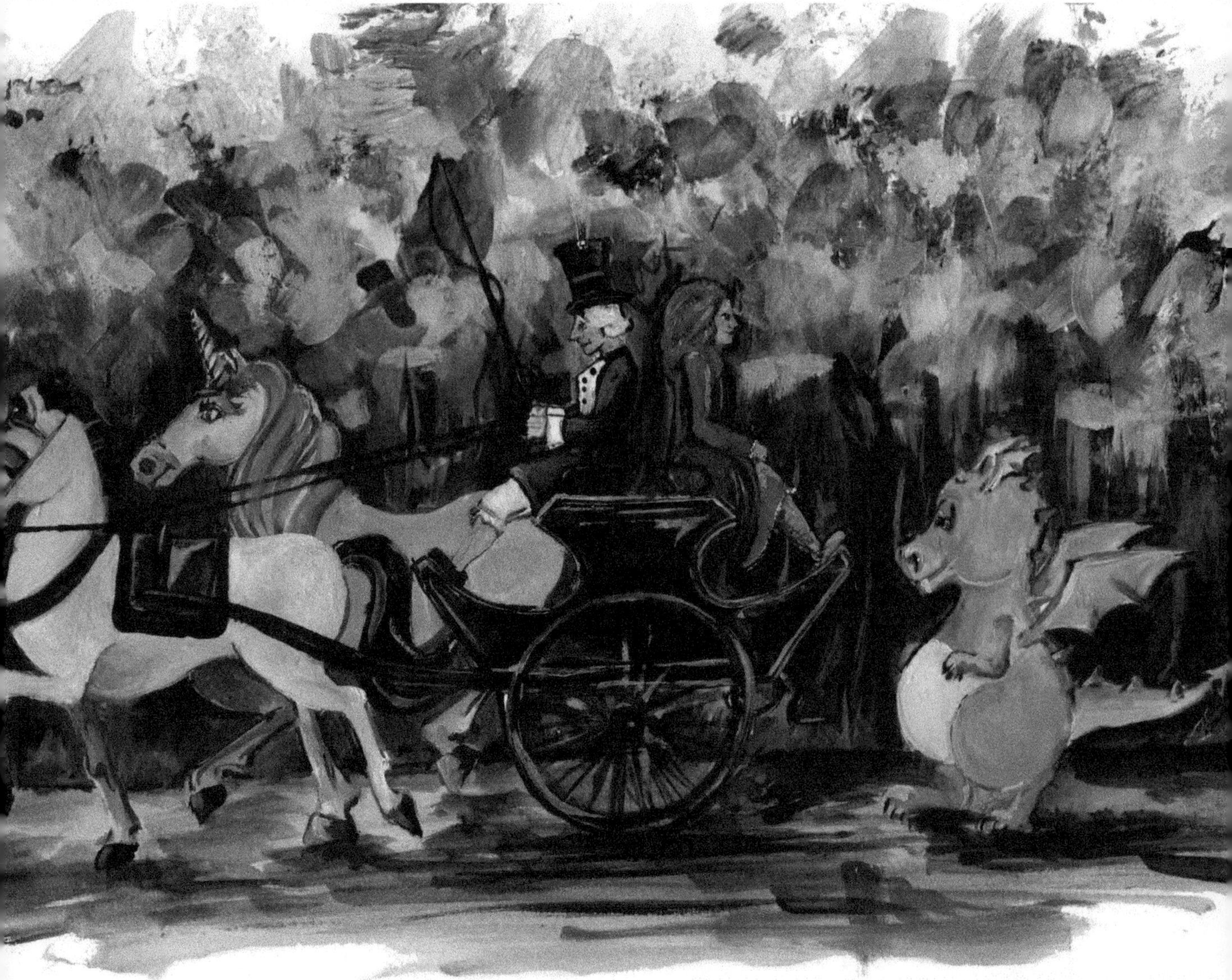

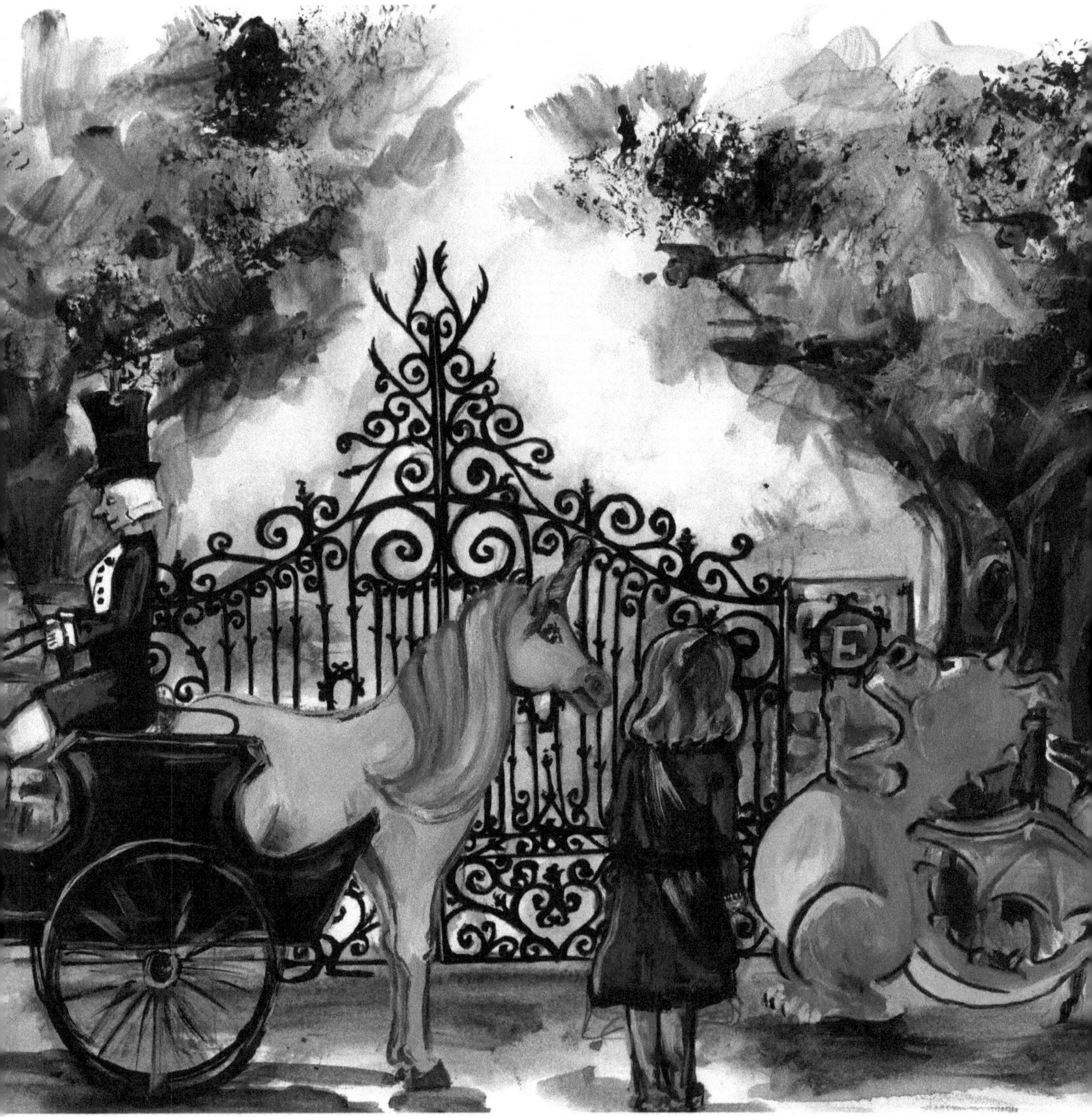
E

The road to the Everett Mansion was bumpy, but they knew they had arrived when they saw an enormous letter "E" carved into the pillar beside the gate.

They proceeded up a steep hill and there, at the very top, was the most beautiful stone mansion one could ever imagine. It was surrounded by tile that matched the color of the turrets. The entryway was carefully arranged cobblestones and there was a cascade of water opposite the main door. It could not have been a more beautiful sight – even better than anything Lady *Lucy*. Dillon and Tapestry could have imagined.

But, there was something strange. The mansion was completely empty. There was not a person in sight. There was not an animal in sight. It was eerily quiet, although strangely, lit lanterns welcomed the threesome on either side of the main entry.

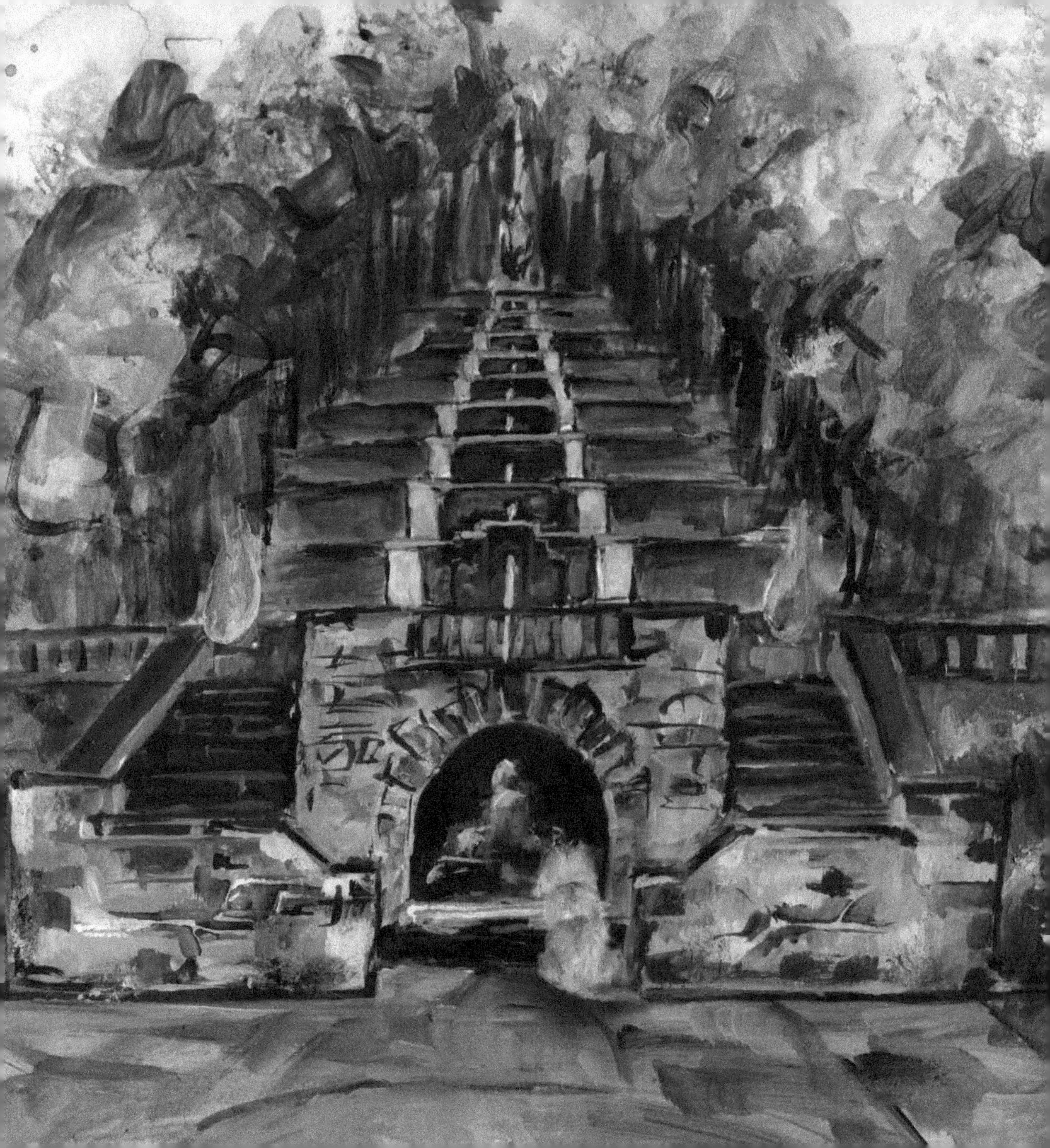

As they walked in the mansion, they were transfixed. The floors were created out of terracotta tiles that glistened with the sunlight flowing through the windows. Then, straight ahead was a stunning ballroom with three lit chandeliers and brass fixtures on the glass doors that encased the room. And looking out from the ballroom, they could see the green mountains and rolling hills of grass. They could not help but pause and absorb the glorious room and views that surrounded them.

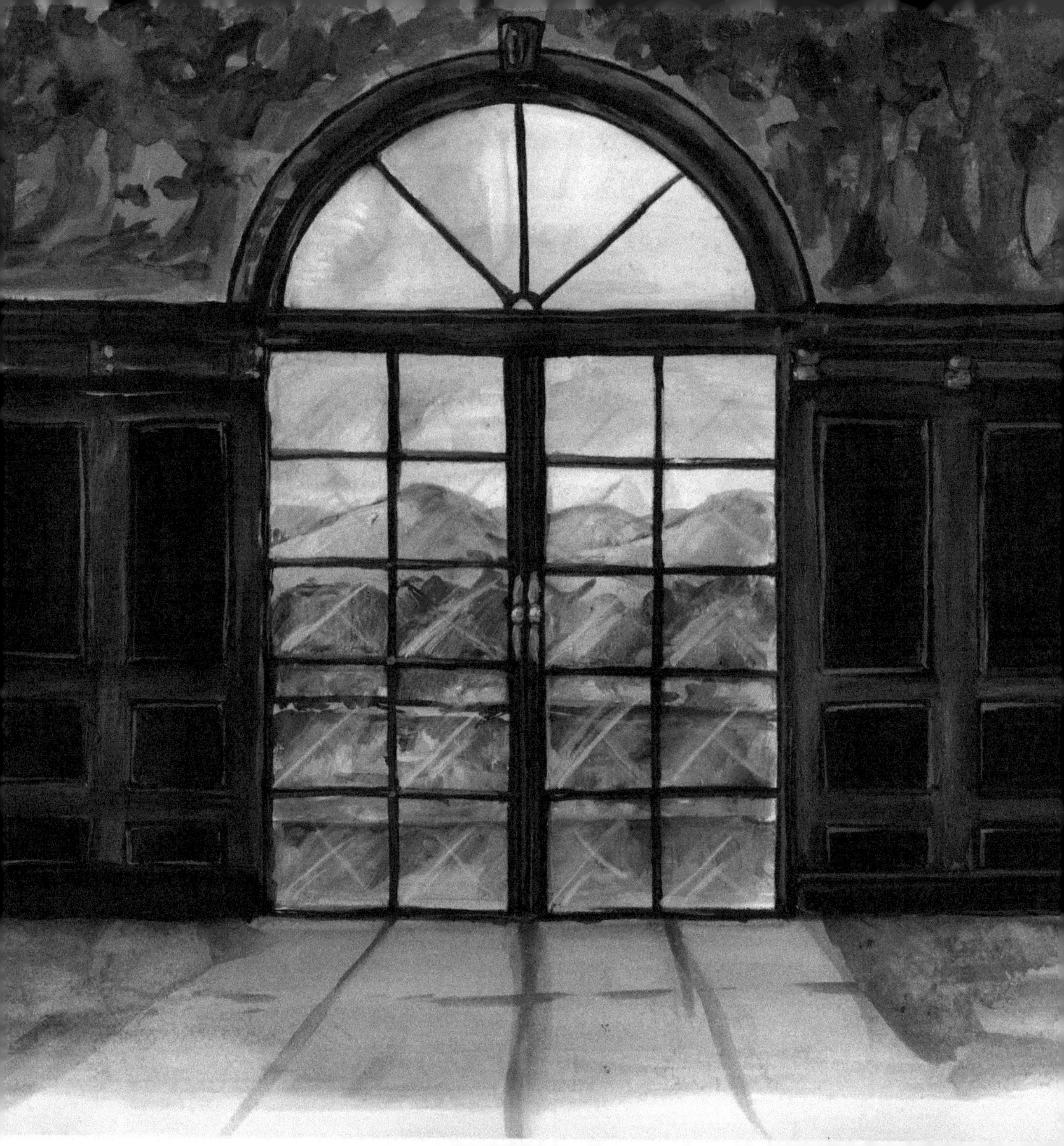

Lady *Lucy* then started to explore the mansion. She saw amazing Turkish tiles; she even saw a tiled bathtub! She saw wall paintings and woodcarvings. She soon called Dillon and Tapestry into a gorgeous wood paneled room with images of the construction of the mansion.

There were illustrations of barren land on which the mansion now stood. There were drawings of horse drawn buggies hauling stone up the hill and master stone layers building the mansion around a well-designed wooden frame.

And, in the far corner of one of the drawings was a family. The father, a rather stout man with a moustache, was sitting on a very large chestnut colored horse. Beside him was a younger looking wife wearing a bonnet and three young girls, all dressed in gingham with their hair in pigtails.

Lady *Lucy* and Tapestry went up the grand stairwell with carved wooden banisters while Dillon explored the dining room with its fabric covered walls and shimmering lights. He was, as always, in search of food. At the top of the stairs, Lady *Lucy* and Tapestry realized that they could climb even higher. So up they went to the third floor, filled with small bedrooms that must have been occupied by the stone layers and cooks and gardeners who kept the mansion looking and functioning perfectly.

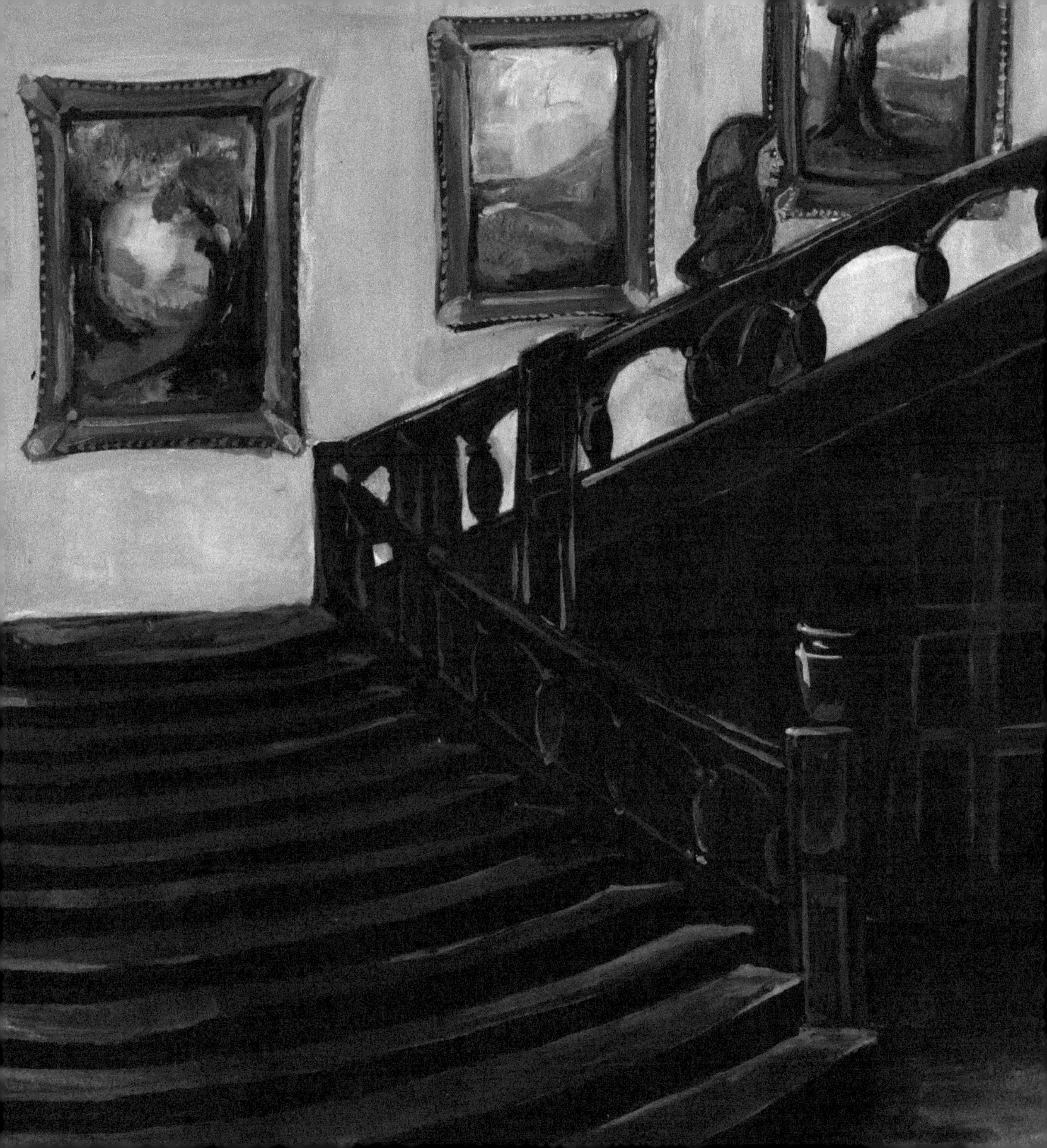

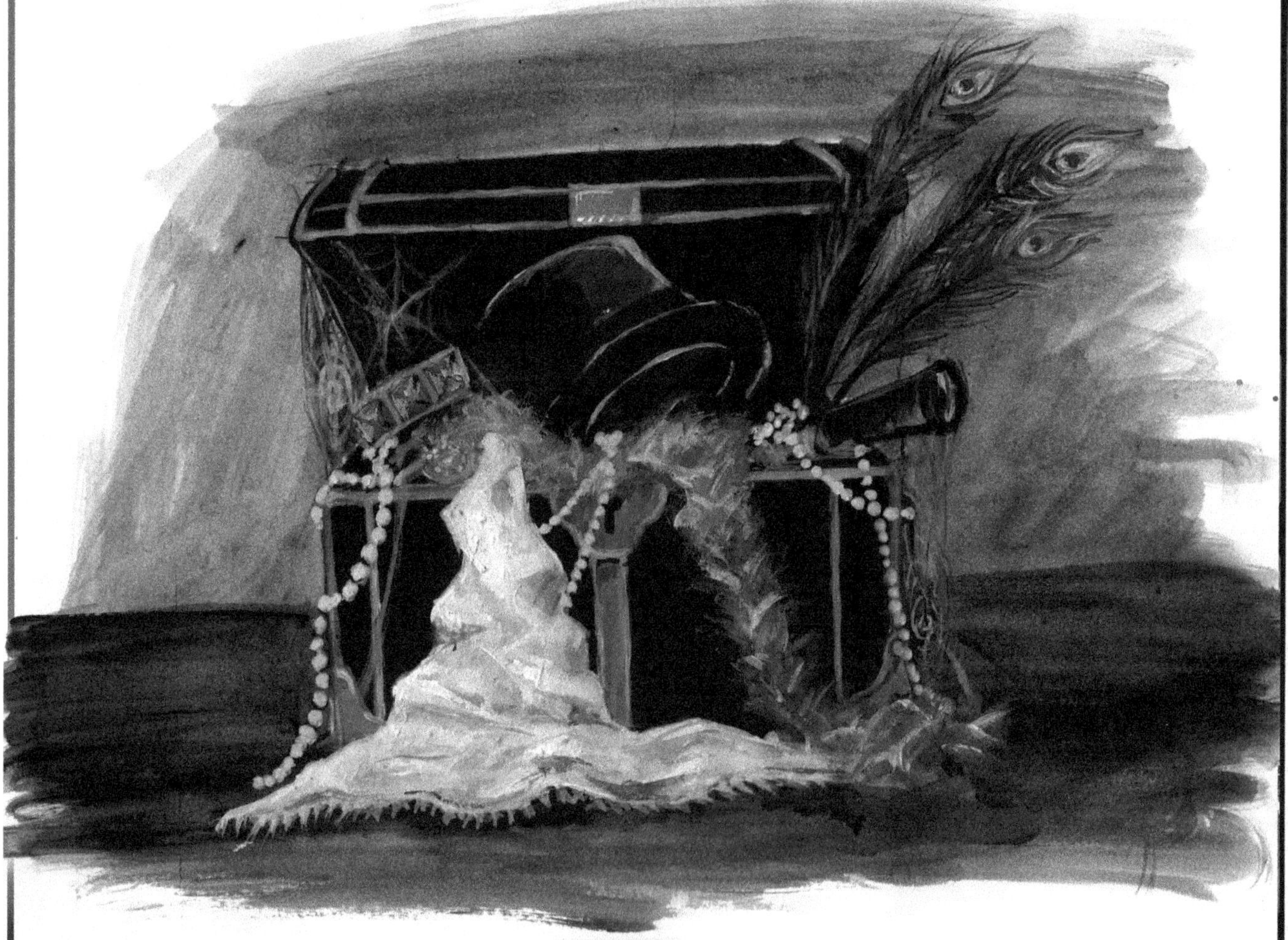

Then, when gazing up at the ceiling on the third floor, Tapestry saw a steel ladder tucked high and she yanked it down with her teeth pulling on a small rope that was dangling. Down fell a small narrow ladder and Lady *Lucy* then climbed up the steel steps, and there was an attic filled with memorabilia: paintings and pottery, furniture and fine china, clothing and curtains and bottles and bottle caps. And last, but not least, there was an enormous tapestry, which Lady *Lucy* lugged down the stairs to show Tapestry, who was sure this tapestry was similar to the one after which she was named.

Their tour of the mansion was extensive and each room held a special treat: a good view, a secret closet, a remarkable brass window opener, a carved doorknob, a marble fireplace, a decorative tile, a hidden letter "E." Lady *Lucy*, Dillon and Tapestry were awestruck but they had an odd feeling too: where was everyone?

It appeared as if the mansion had been abandoned in a hurry – as if the occupants scurried off the premises as if they were being chased.

As they bedded down for the night in the central ballroom, Tapestry was the first to speak. "How will we know if there are ghosts? Do you think the ghosts will know we are here? How do we know if these are the friendly kind of ghosts?" As she asked these questions, she started shivering and her eyes lit up and her mane and tail flailed.

Lady *Lucy* calmly said: "If we are together, the ghosts can't scare us. And, let's try asking the ghosts to join us and sit with us and talk with us."

At that point, Dillon reared his head and said, "I'll talk to a ghost. That will be fun. They probably have never seen a creature as big and colorful as me."

All three looked at each other, realizing that much could happen in the night ahead but they had each other for protection and encouragement and off to sleep they went.

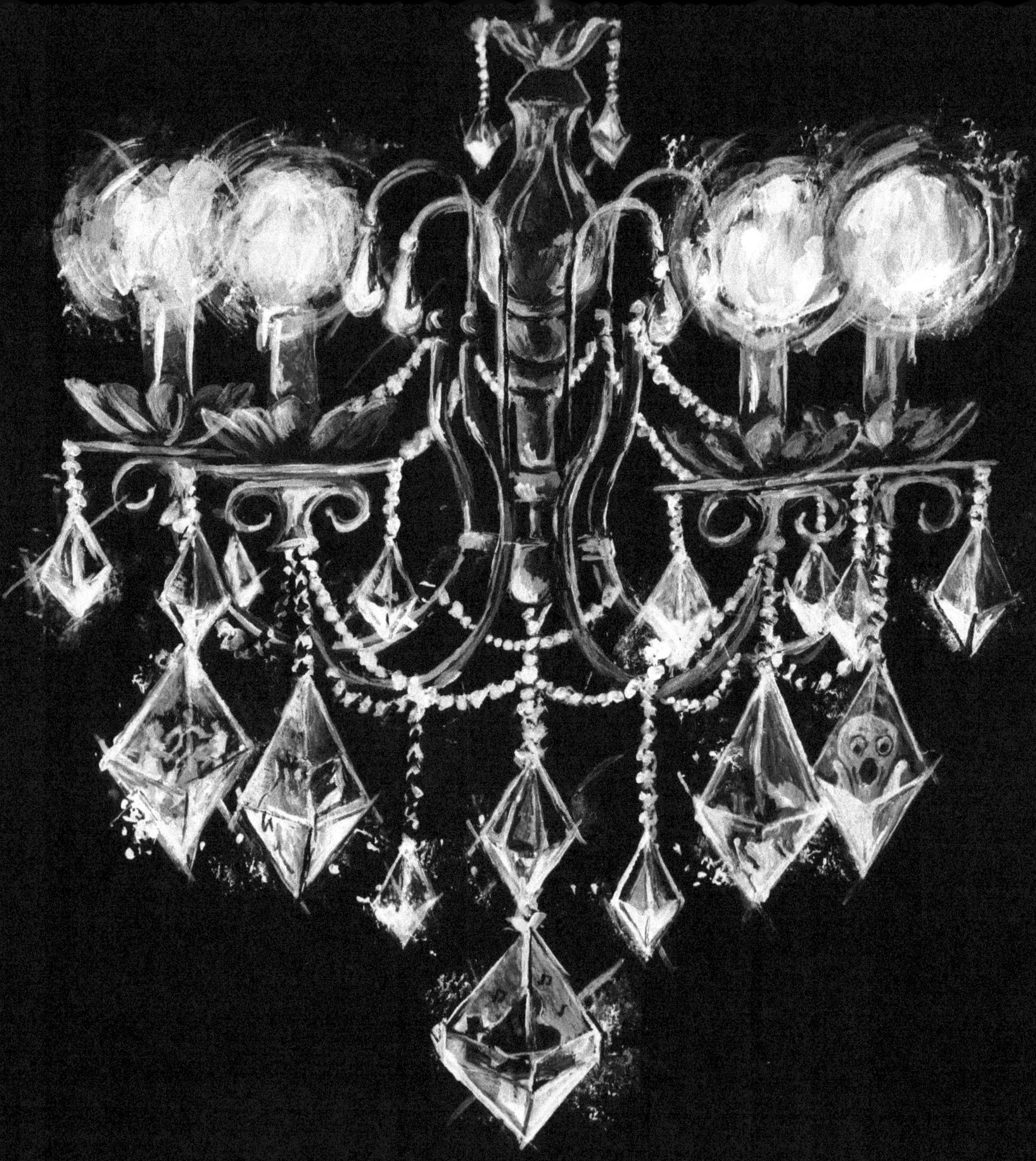

Shortly after the threesome fell asleep, they were awakened by flicking in the chandeliers over their heads. "Hmm," they all thought and fell back to sleep. The next morning, Lady *Lucy*, Dillon and Tapestry were exhausted. They all had boisterous or terrible dreams. "I heard children laughing and playing all night," said Lady *Lucy*. "I saw Mr. Everett slung sideways over a horse galloping across the lawn, back and forth, back and forth," said Tapestry. "I heard screams of someone in the attic near the metal stairs and she screamed all night," said Dillon. Together they shared that they heard a piano being played throughout the night.

The threesome decided they were all dreaming but just to be sure, they decided to look inside and outside the mansion to see if there was any evidence of children, horses, a piano player or a woman in the attic. They looked everywhere and could not find one single shred of evidence of anything that they heard or saw in the night. They all agreed, "We were dreaming."

The next night, Lady *Lucy*, Dillon and Tapestry agreed to try to stay awake all night. But, as the hours passed, they fell sound asleep. They awoke with a startle and looked at each other. "I dreamt there was a big party here, with all sorts of people dressed in fancy clothes," said Lady *Lucy*. "That's strange," said Dillon, "I had the same dream. People were dancing and enjoying this ballroom as the candles glowed." "This is totally bizarre," said Tapestry. "I had the identical dream and the people were all so happy in the mansion, enjoying each other, the setting and the scenery and soft piano music."

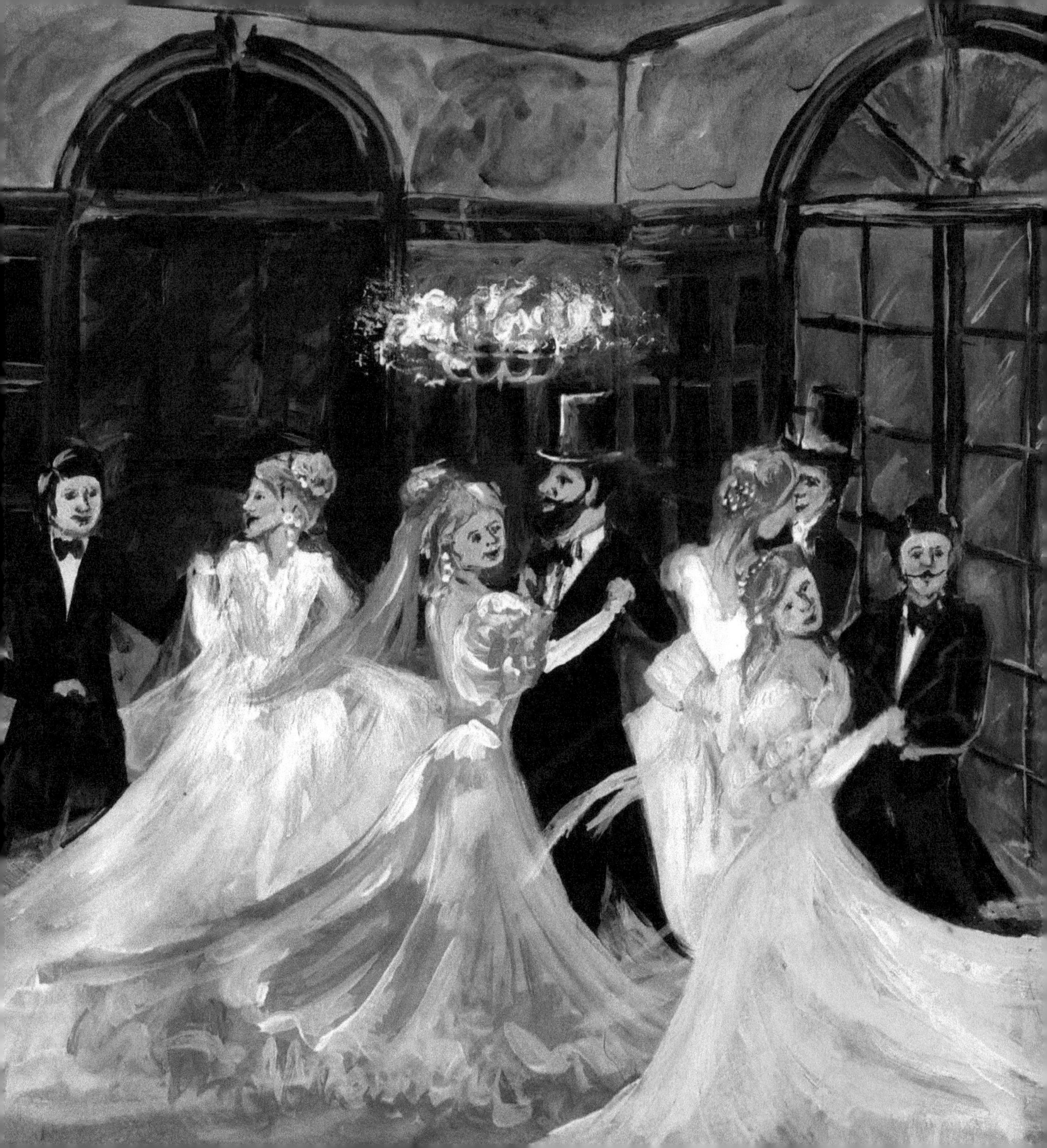

They all agreed to look inside and outside the mansion for evidence of a huge party, with music and food and dancing and elegant clothing. No matter where they looked, they could not find even a scintilla of proof that there had been a glorious party. There was no food or drink anywhere to Dillon's disappointment. There were no fancy clothes or sparkling shoes or jewelry to Tapestry's disappointment.

There was no evidence of any person --- no footprints, no lost items left behind, no decorations to Lady *Lucy's* disappointment. There was a lone out-of-tune piano hidden in a corner.

The threesome started to think: Could there have been ghosts and they were having a party? Was the party real? A real ghost party? Impossible. Unlikely. Certainly unusual.

By now, Lady *Lucy*, Dillon and Tapestry were frustrated. They were on a mission to save the mansion and so far, they had not met any real people, and the mansion was largely empty except in the attic and the many books in the library. And, every night, the threesome had unusual dreams that seemed real but there was never a single bit of evidence to support the reality of what they imagined.

The third night, Lady *Lucy* suggested they each sleep in a different room, hoping for a different outcome. Tapestry was not pleased. She liked sleeping in the big ballroom and she was always a little afraid of change. Dillon suggested they sleep outside so they could see the stars and who was coming and going into the mansion. Lady *Lucy* suggested they sleep in the library. She liked being surrounded by books and thought perhaps some of the knowledge in them could be transported into her head just by being near the rows and rows of books. She just had a feeling that the library would yield some needed information about the mansion.

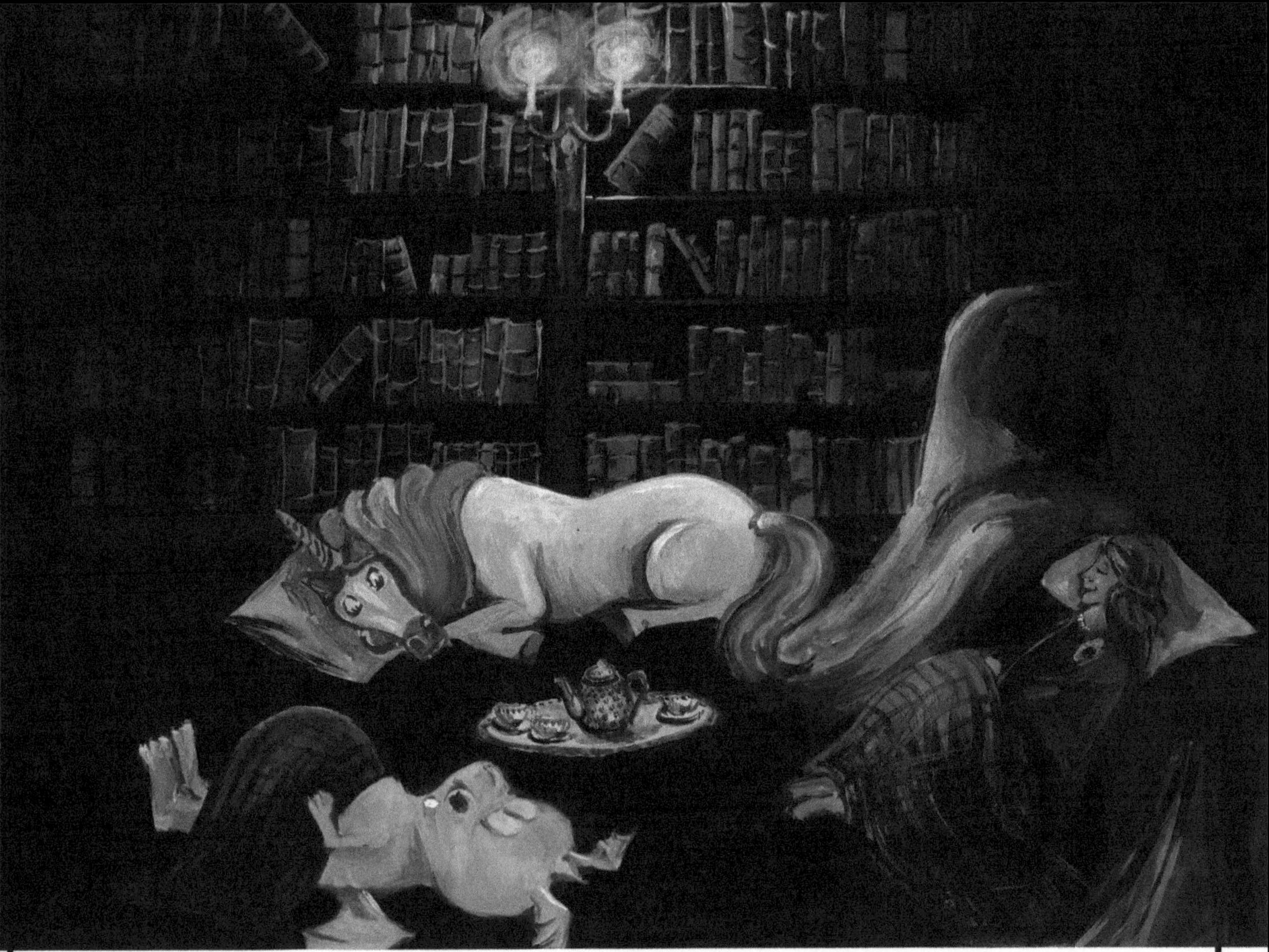

Lady Lucy convinced her two friends that the library was the best place to rest for the night. Believing in Lady Lucy and her instincts, Dillon and Tapestry agreed to bed down for the night in the library. The threesome, after sharing some tea together, went to sleep in the book filled cloth covered library.

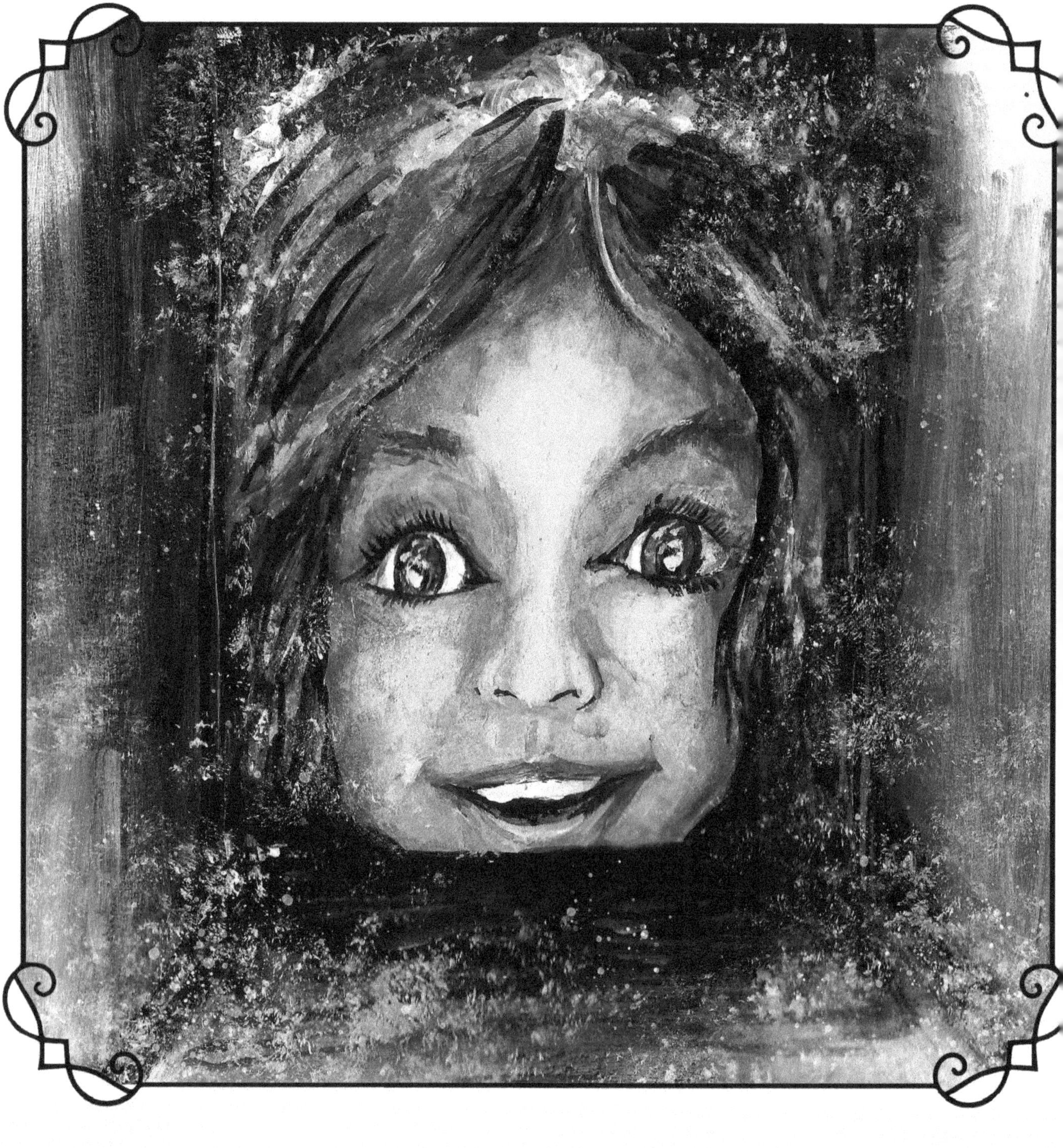

That night, when the three visitors from the County of Heraldshire fell asleep, the strangest thing happened. Several books fell off a shelf near the window in a loud clunk and in their space was a light… a light so bright that it woke up Lady *Lucy*, Dillon and Tapestry. At first they stared at the light, their eyes squinting because of its brightness. It was actually painful to look directly into the light.

Lady *Lucy* decided to approach the light. "Be careful," said Dillon. "You could get burned if the light is hot." "Be cautious," said Tapestry. "You could get pulled into the light and disappear into the wall." Lady *Lucy* agreed as she was worried the light might damage her eyes. She moved slowly and as she approached the light, the space near it got wider and wider until she could see an enormous metal box. She reached her hand inside and touched the box; it seemed real.

She asked Dillon to help her lift the box out of the wall and together they placed it on the floor. "Don't open it," shouted Tapestry. "It could contain poison." "We'll open it carefully," said Lady *Lucy* as she and Dillon lifted the heavy metal lid to the box. And as soon as the lid was opened, a golden glow emerged, and when the lid was totally removed, they saw what seemed like millions of pieces of gold. The coins were shiny and glistened.

The threesome stared at the box filled with riches. Someone or something had wanted them to find all this money in the library, money that could save the Everett Mansion.

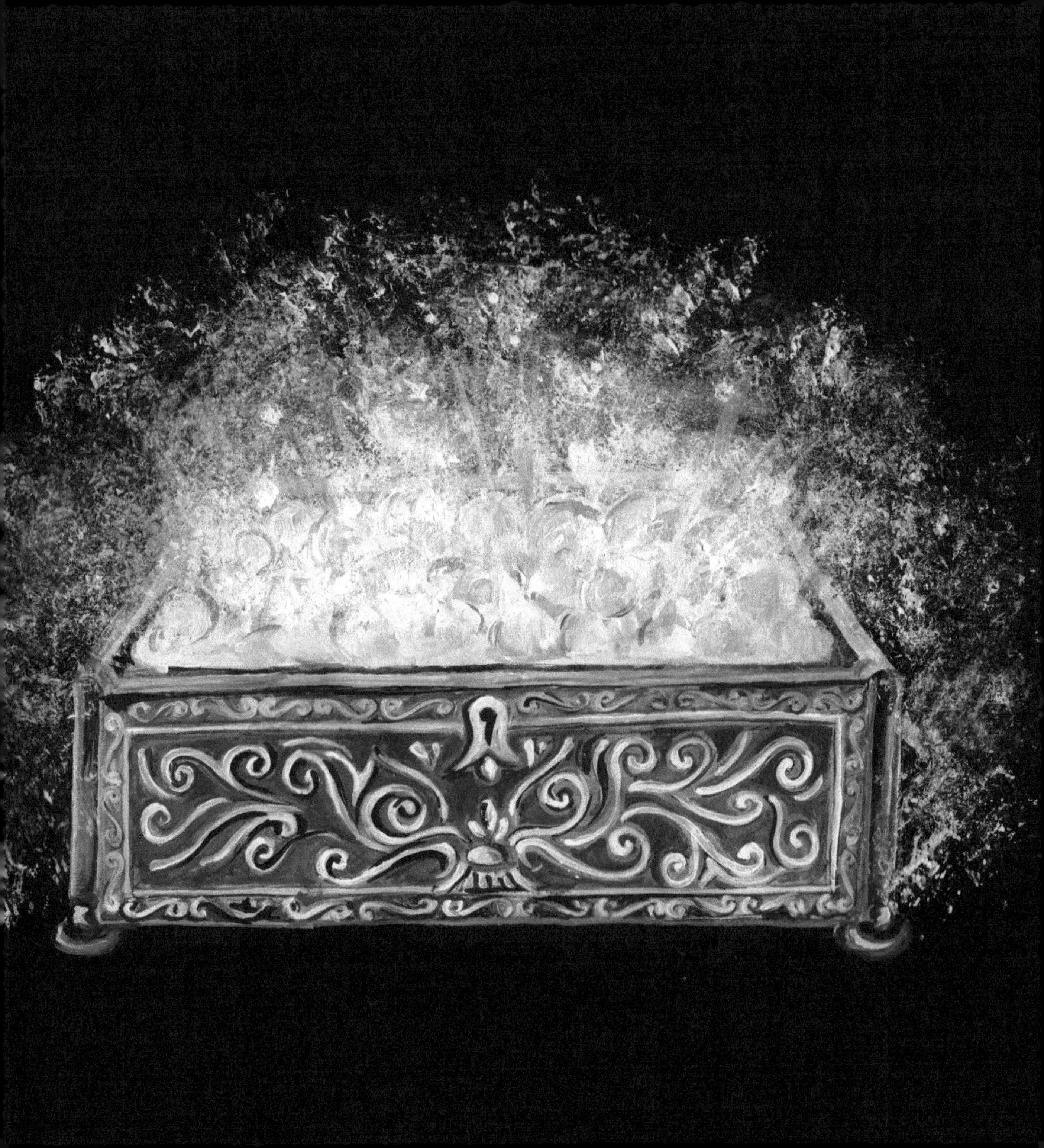

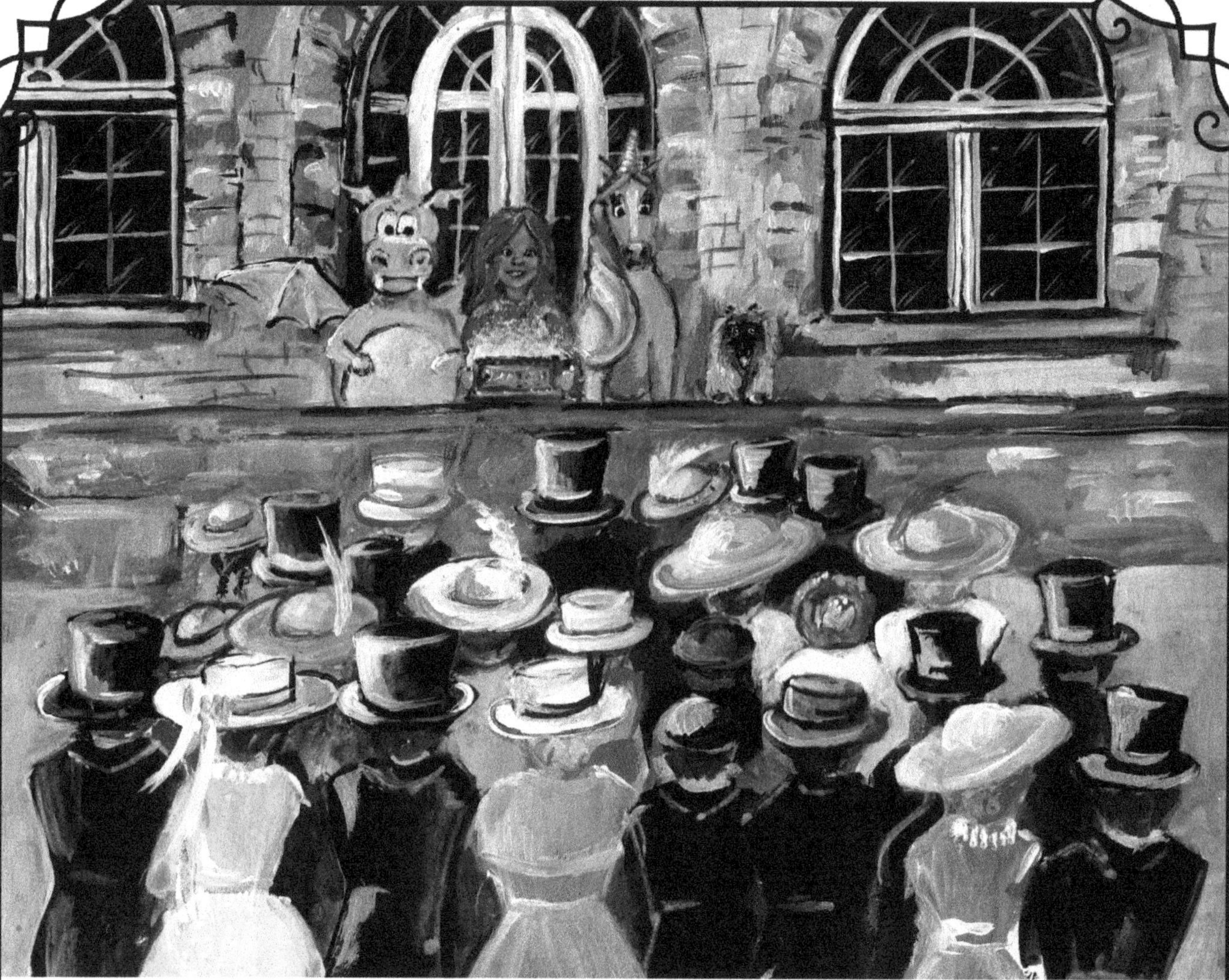

With a bugle, Lady *Lucy* called out to all the townspeople of Vermont and asked them to gather on the mansion lawn at high noon. Even Dillon and Tapestry did not know what Lady *Lucy* was going to say.

By noon, hundreds of people arrived at the mansion and sat on the lawn, looking left and right and in front and behind them because they were so scared and unsure as to what was happening.

Lady *Lucy*, surrounded by Dillon and Tapestry, emerged from the mansion. She introduced herself and explained that she and her friends, whom she also introduced, had traveled from far away to save the Everett Mansion. And, she was pleased to announce that she had come upon a salvation strategy. Quickly and with Dillon's help, she unveiled the steel chest filled with gold and explained that the threesome had found the money in the library.

Lady *Lucy* then pronounced:

"Since the gold was found in the library, I have come to realize that the way to save the mansion is to make it a place of knowledge, a place where children of all ages can come to learn. They can learn about science and literature. They can learn about music and dance. They can learn about history and anatomy. They can learn about animals and nature. They can learn about geography. They can even learn about the mansion's past including ghosts and Mr. Everett's successful bottle cap business."

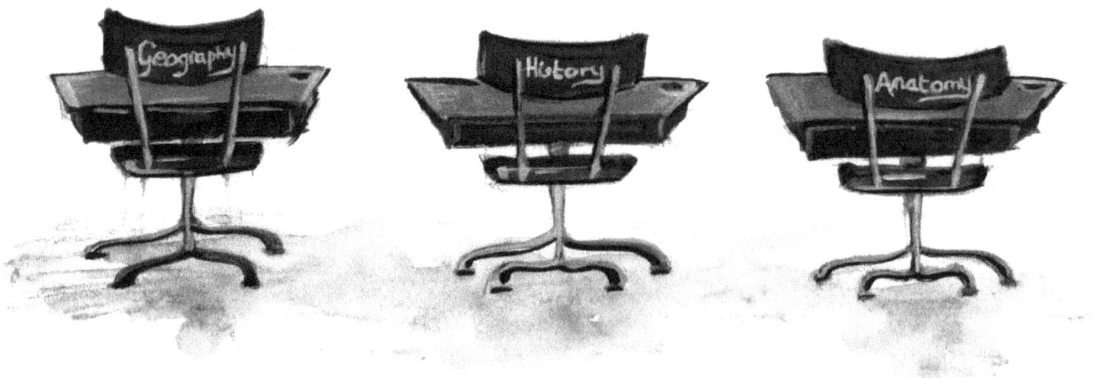
Geography
History
Anatomy

Lady *Lucy*, Dillon and Tapestry could not help but overhear the whispers. Quieting the crowd, each of the three visitors spoke. Lady *Lucy* said, "I appreciate that you are scared; I was scared too when I arrived here. But, the mansion is sending all of us a message; it is a place of learning where the library is the center of the school." Then she added, "This mansion is an amazing place to learn. What better place could there be to gain information and ask questions, all while enjoying the most beautiful setting in Vermont --- perhaps in the whole world?"

Dillon then chimed in, "I have seen many scary places and spaces and this mansion is not one of them. If I were scared, I would be able to blow water or fire for protection and I don't need to do either. The mansion is filled with a generosity of spirit and it is now welcoming all creatures, large and small, human and animal alike."

Then Tapestry stepped forward and in a quiet shy voice she added, "I was worried about ghosts also. I am a careful creature. But here is what I have learned. There are good ghosts, ghosts that help us, ghosts that guide us, ghosts that enable us to envision a good future. These are the kind of ghosts inhabiting Everett Mansion."

All the townspeople listened and as they did, the sun shone, the gold glistened and Tapestry's glorious tail and mane lit up like sparkling stars. They felt welcomed and comforted and one by one, two by two, they entered the mansion for the first time in a long, long time. And so it was that the townspeople worked together and the mansion became a successful school.

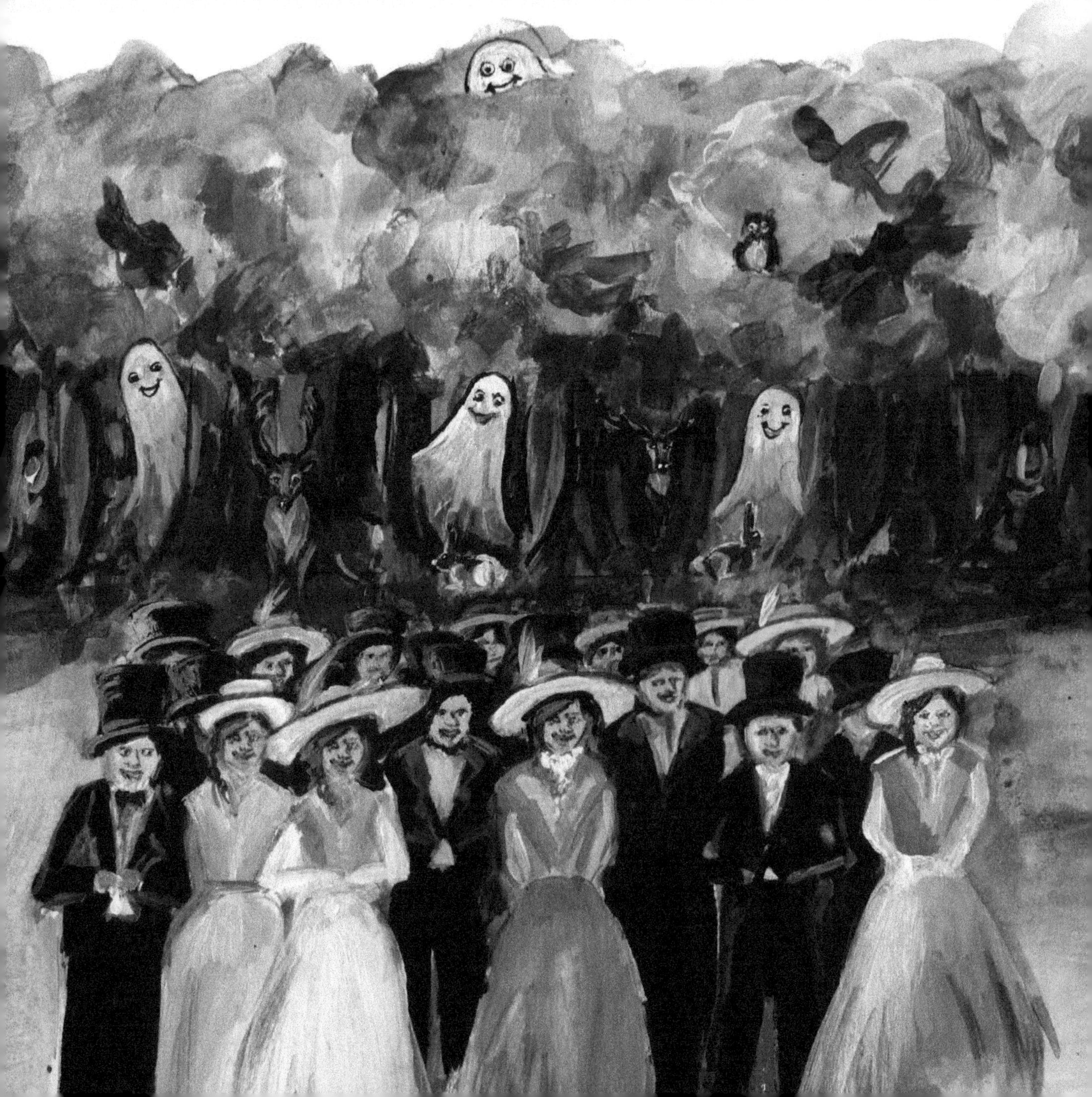

With little ceremony, Lady *Lucy*, Dillon and Tapestry returned to their homeland. And, back in Heraldshire, Lady *Lucy*, Dillon and Tapestry shared stories of the school at Everett Mansion and there was joy in the land. And, over the coming decades, many children from Heraldshire traveled to the Everett Mansion to spend time learning in Vermont.

And, the iron wrought letter "E" at the entrance of the mansion on the iron gate became known as the "Everett Education E" and throughout the mansion and Vermont and everywhere in the world when people saw the letter "E," they recalled that it stood for "Everett Education," the education that was started and carried out in an amazing mansion in Vermont.

And sometimes, only sometimes, if the light is just right, you could see a dog right next to that "E," the same dog Dillon spotted all those years ago.

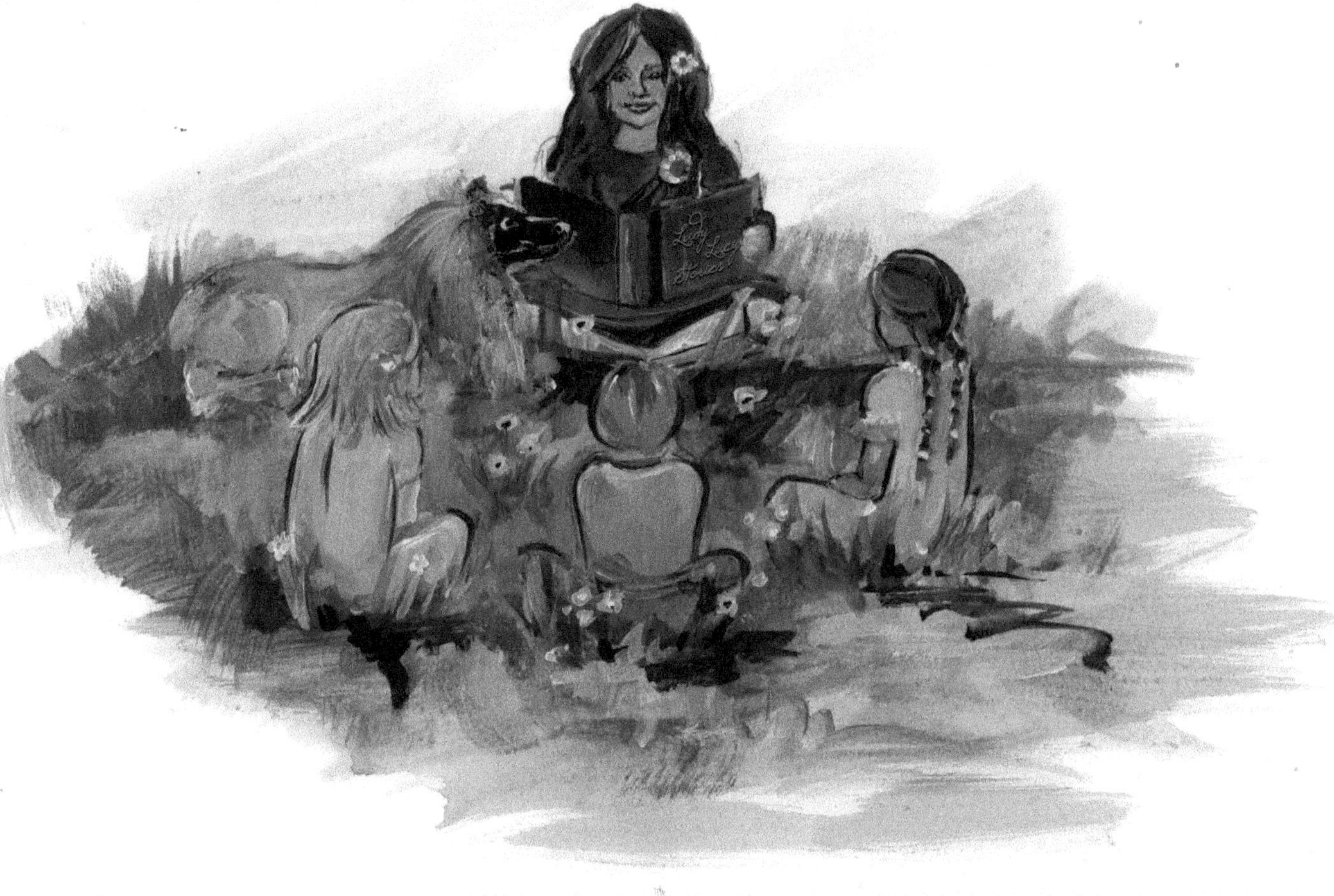

Karen Gross

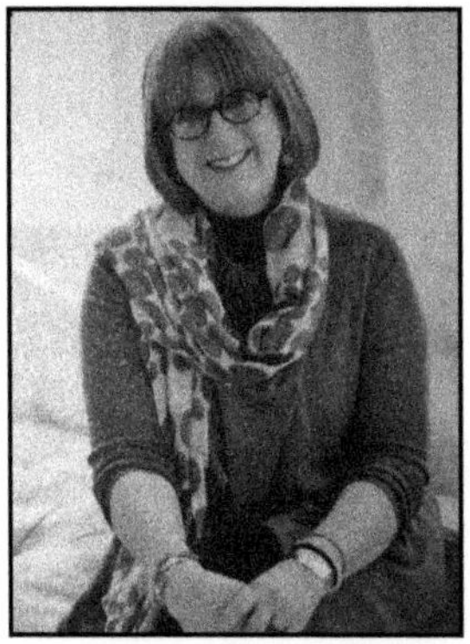

Karen Gross is an author, educator and storyteller. Previously, she was president of Southern Vermont College in Bennington, VT and served as a Senior Policy Advisor to the US Department of Education. Prior to that, she was a law professor for 2 decades focusing on asset building in low income communities. Currently, she is Senior Counsel to Finn Partners where she specializes in crisis management. An expert in trauma and disaster planning and relief, she is certified as a PFA provider (Psychological First Aid) and enrolled in a clinical certification program in trauma at the Rutgers Graduate School of Social Work. She has a forthcoming adult book published by Columbia Teachers College Press on how to ameliorate trauma and foster improved student success across the educational landscape. She resides in Washington, DC, home to some fish and lots of swamps.

Other Books by Karen Gross:

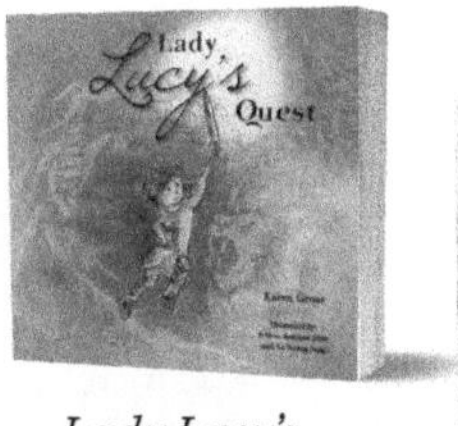
Lady Lucy's Quest

Lady Lucy's Quest

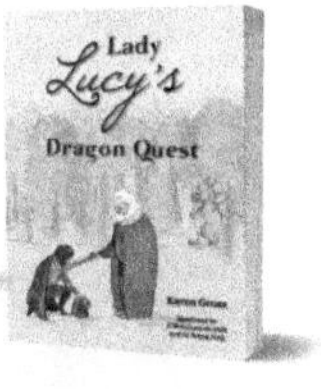
Lady Lucy's
Dragon Quest

Lady Lucy's Dragon Quest

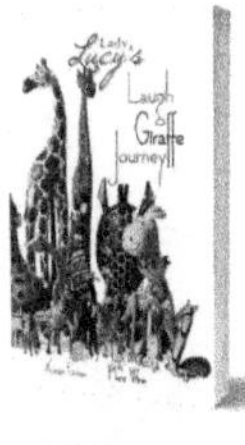
Lady Lucy's

Lady Lucy's Laugh Giraffe Journey

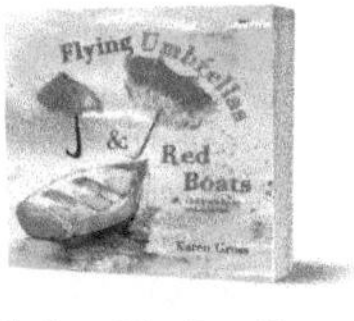
Flying Umbrellas
& Red Boats

Flying Umbrellas & Red Boats

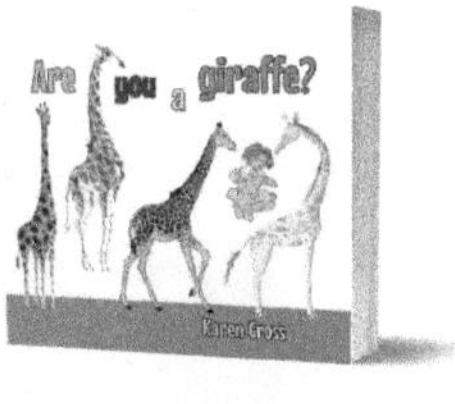
Are you a giraffe?

Are you a giraffe?

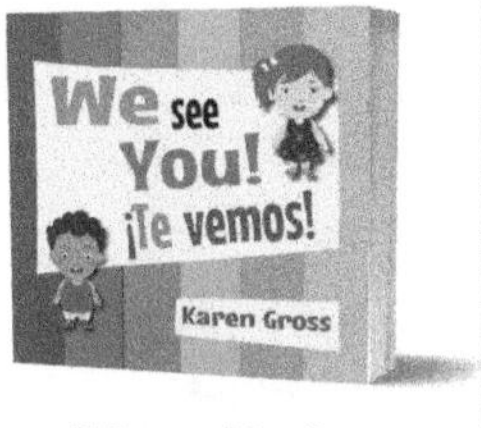
We see You!
¡Te vemos!
Karen Gross

We see You! !Te vemos!

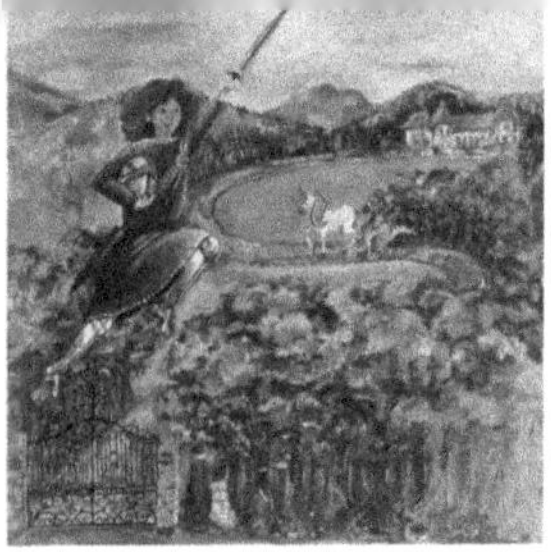
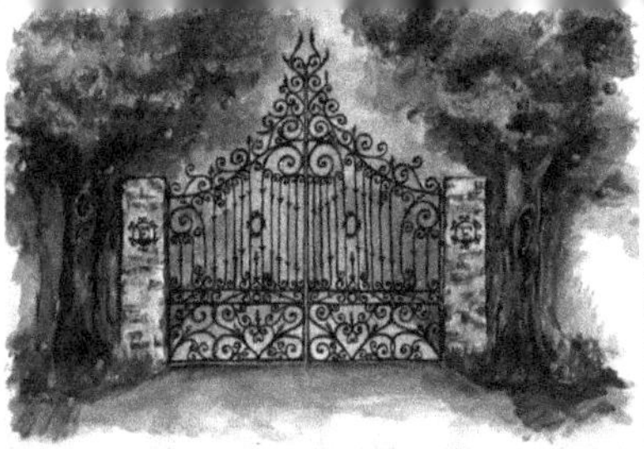
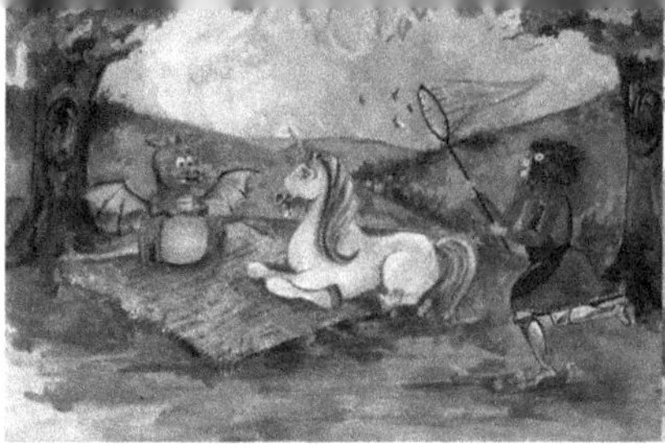
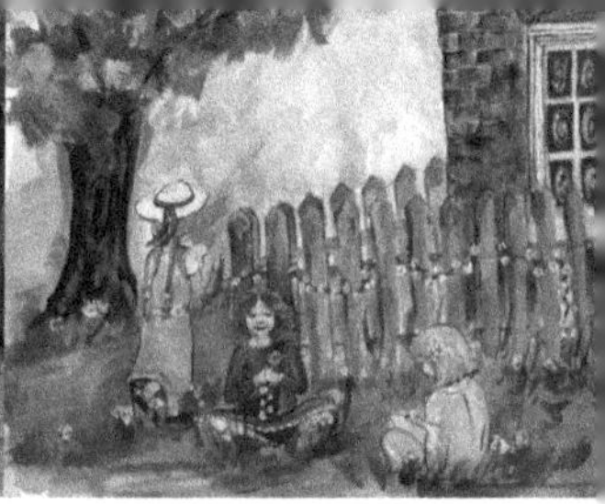
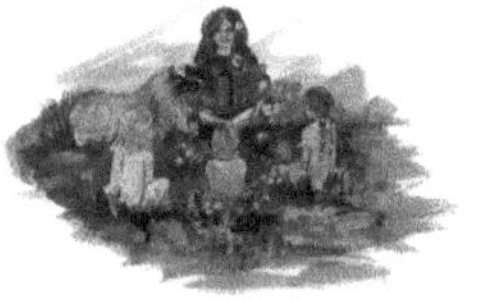

Illustrator: Georgia Hamp

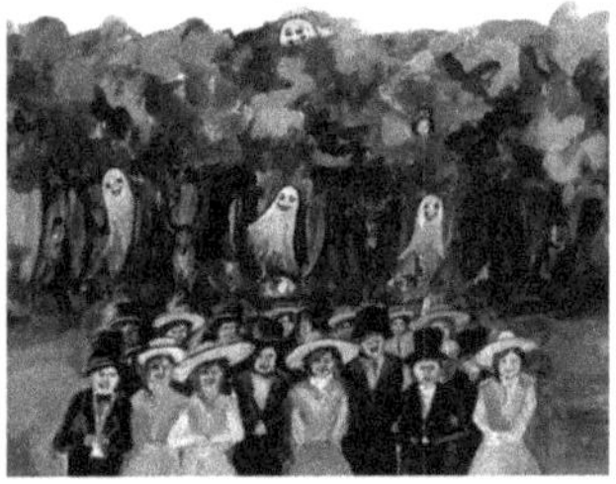
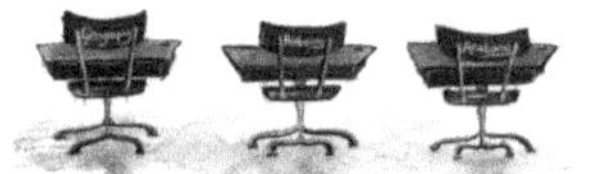
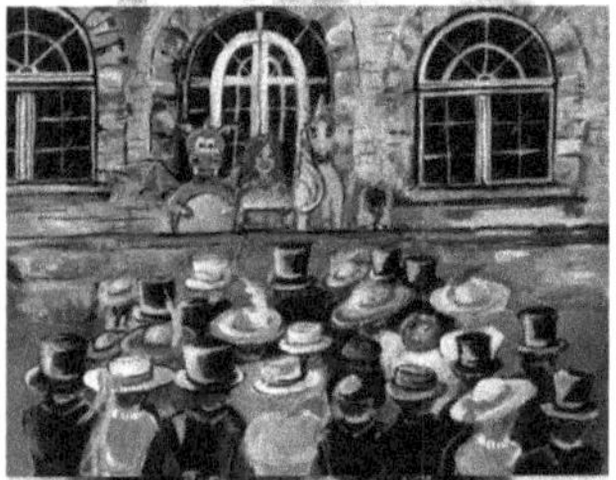
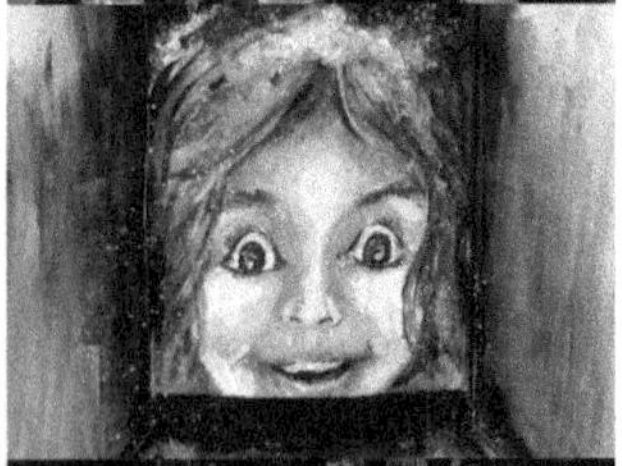
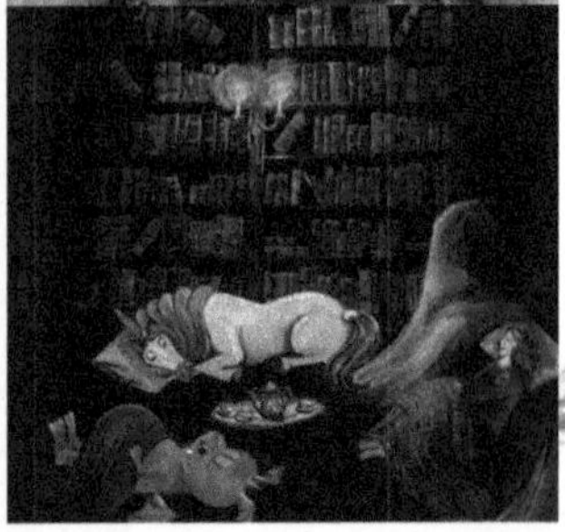

Georgia Hamp was born in Ockley Surrey England and studied Art History and Architecture at University. She was recognised early as a very talented illustrator and team player, supporting graphic design projects and publications.

Her love of Art History proved very valuable to the *Lady Lucy Ghost Quest*. Dianne introduced her to the Edwardian Art work of John S. Goodhall. With excellent visual literacy, she analysed the images and the objects of the time.

Georgia's experience as a student of Architecture was incredibly valuable to the story. One will never forget her illustration of the Everett Estate Cascade! Also, her experience, working with designers embellished the intelligence of the designs presented to her. Imagine being confronted with the design plan of placing parts of the story in the crystals of the chandelier! Georgia's ability to effectively surpass the design briefs proved to be incredibly complimentary to one of the most memorable stories.

Indeed, as an artistic team player, Georgia's talent supported the dedication of the Lucy Quest stories with an impressive recreation of the splendid architecture and era, along with the visions of hope; past, present and future.

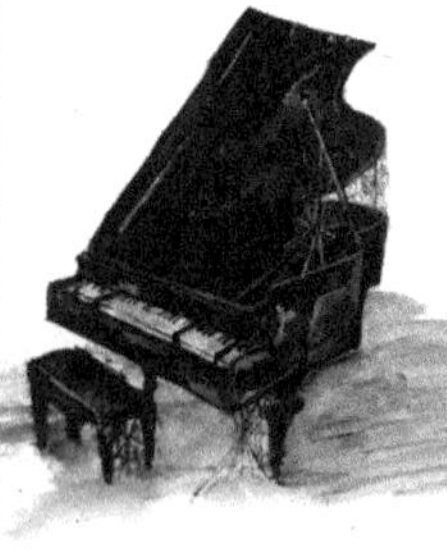
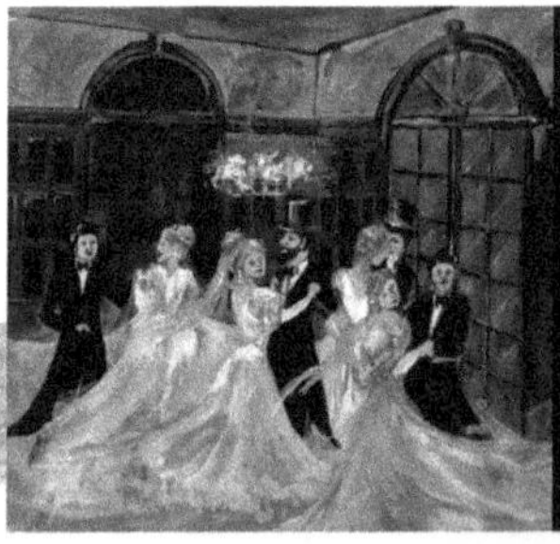
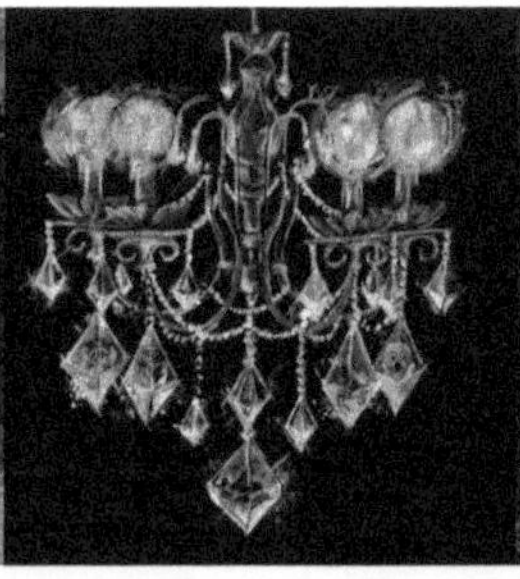
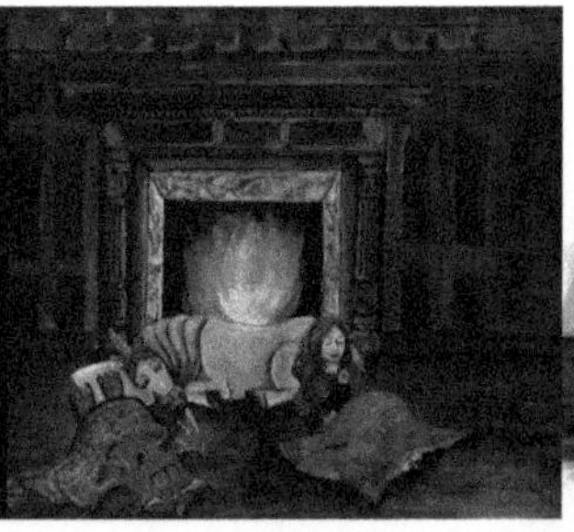

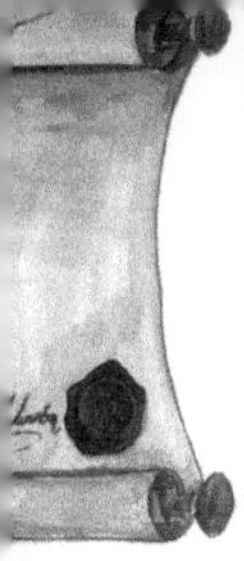
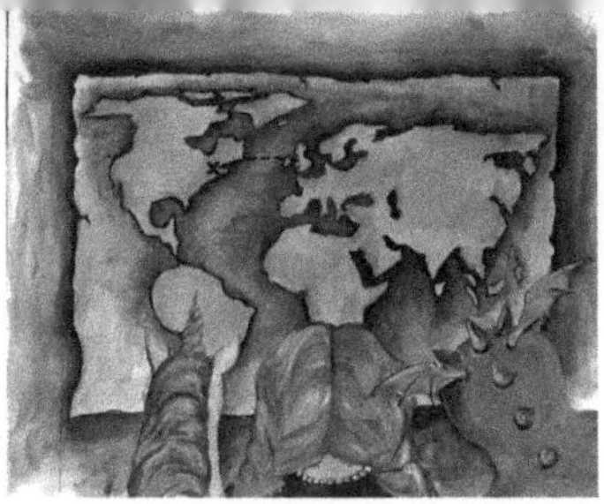
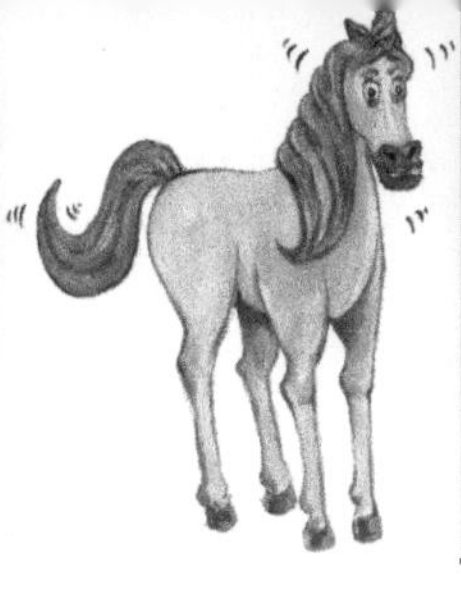
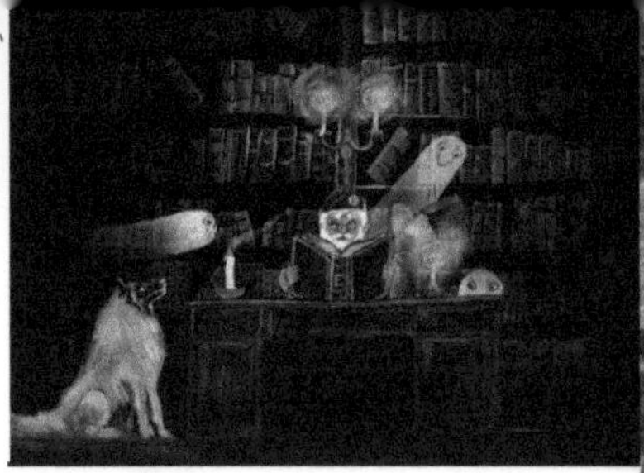
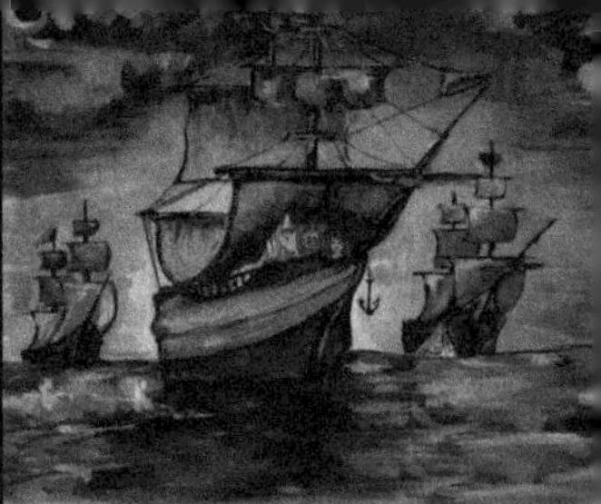

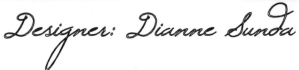

Designer: Dianne Sunda

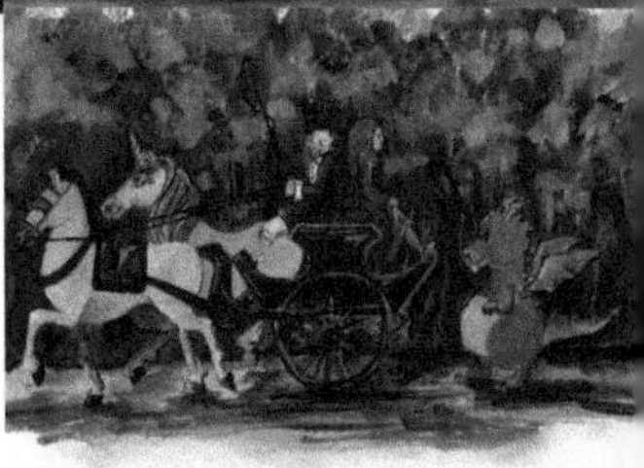

Dianne Sunda was born in Nyack, New York and began her artistic career while at university in America and in Belgium. She currently designs botanical art for historic buildings, while writing articles about gardens and garden history. Dianne published her early books while serving international trade programs.

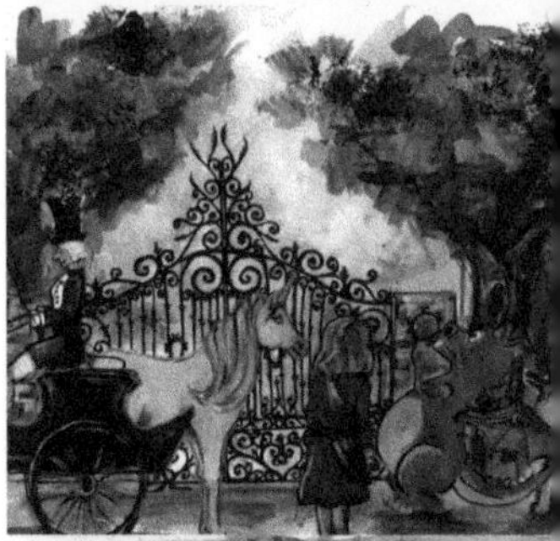

Dianne has bestowed a wealth of educational curriculum development to her current role as founder of the International Children's Museum Foundation (an innovative in-kind sponsorship foundation). Dianne designed and wrote the book: LETTERS TO THE ANIMALS, which is a download from the Foundation website. Every Christmas, she writes a Christmas story for children for online publication. Dianne continues to teach Art for her Foundation. Her Family Saturday art classes are very popular and she also mentors aspiring artists and writers of all ages.

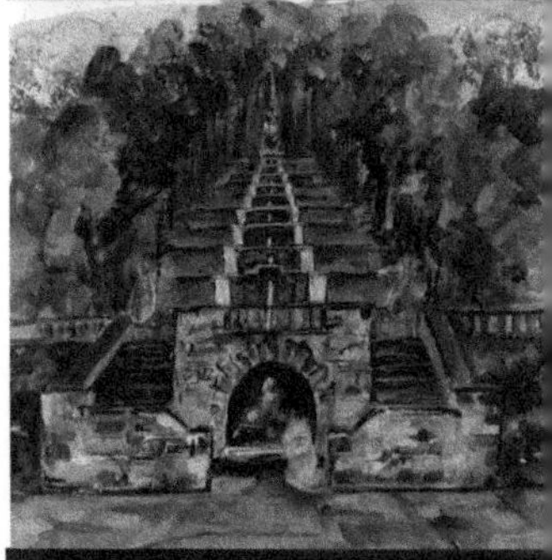

This truly classic story: LADY LUCY'S GHOST QUEST is a remarkable celebration of valued learning experiences that took place at the Everett Estate; an Estate close to Dianne's heart. Dianne helped Southern Vermont College as one of the founder instructors and remained and developed the four year Liberal Arts program as Dean and Provost during a tenure of ten years.

The illustrator, Georgia Hamp, was recognised quickly by Dianne's Foundation when she was a student as one of the most gifted illustrators. Their teamwork has, indeed, complimented one of the most inspirational stories, bestowing the potential of impassioned literature.

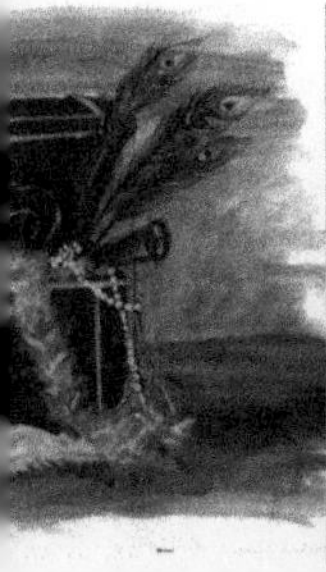
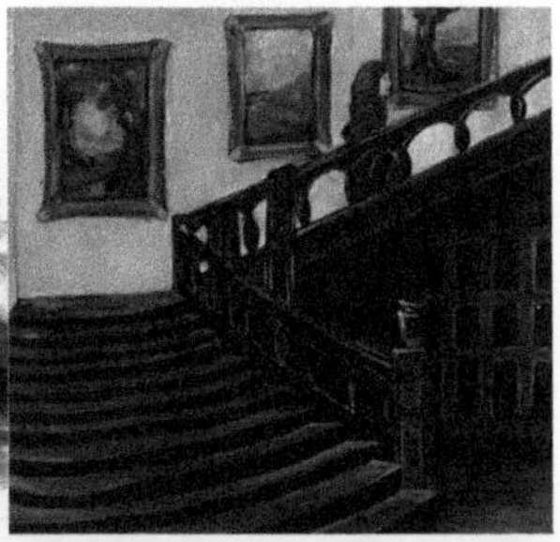
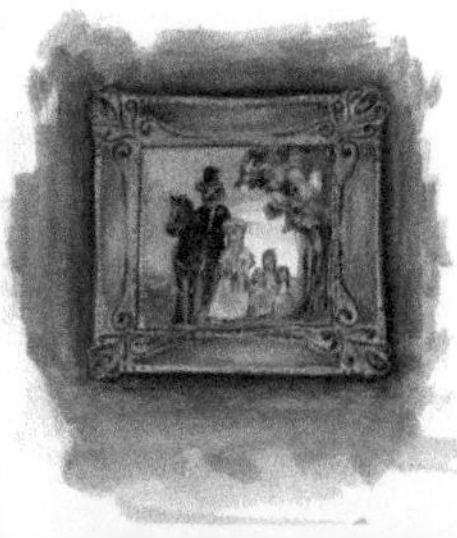
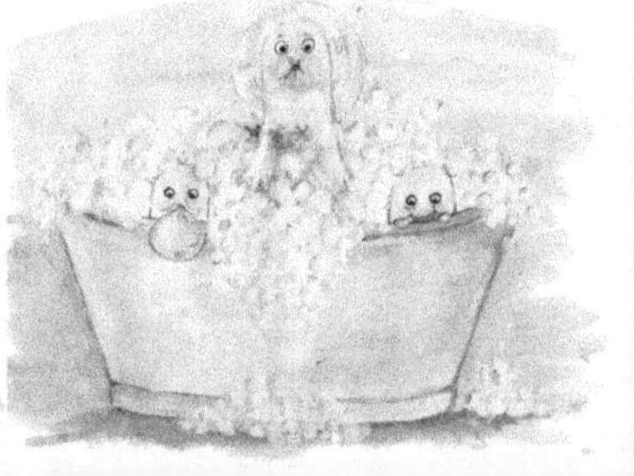
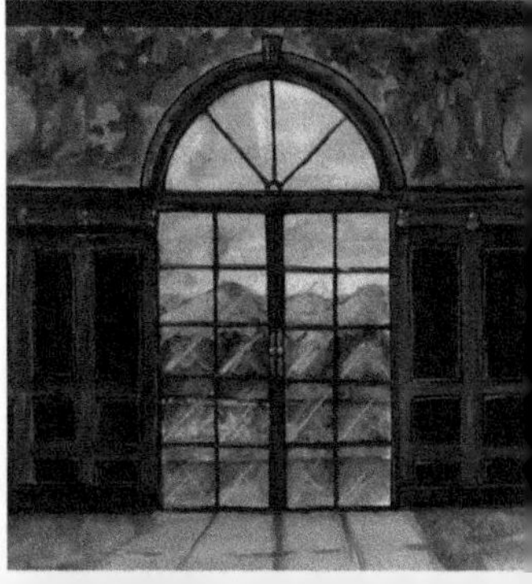

CPSIA information can be obtained
at www.ICGtesting.com
Printed in the USA
JSHW022138301019
2166JS00001B/1

9 781605 715094